Praise for Robert Asprin's Myth Adventures series

"Asprin's major achievement as a writer—brisk pacing, wit, and a keen satirical eye. Breezy, pun-filled fantasy in the vein of Piers Anthony's *Xanth* series"—ALA *Booklist*

"A hilarious bit of froth and frolic. Asprin has a fine time with the story. So will the reader."—*Library Journal*

"Witty, humorous, a pleasant antidote to ponderous fantasy." —*Amazing*

"The novels by Asprin are loads of fun, extremely enjoyable humorous fantasy. We really like it."—*The Comic Buyers Guide*

"…an excellent, lighthearted fantasy series…"—*Epic Illustrated*

"An inspired series of magic and hilarity. It's a happy meeting of L. Sprague de Camp and the *Hitchhiker's Guide* trilogy." —*Burlington County Times*

"Humorous adventure fantasy at its rowdiest." —*Science Fiction Chronicle*

"Recommended."—*Fantasy Review*

"All the *Myth* books are hysterically funny."—*Analog*

"This is a fun read and series enthusiasts should enjoy it." —*Kliatt*

Myth-ion Improbable

by

Robert Lynn Asprin

Meisha Merlin Publishing, Inc.
Atlanta, GA

MYTH-ION IMPROBABLE

An MM Publishing Book
Published by Meisha Merlin Publishing, Inc.
PO Box 7
Decatur, GA   30031

Editing & interior layout by Stephen Pagel
Copyediting & proofreading by Josh Mitchell
Cover art by Hoaug
Cover design by Neil Seltzer

ISBN: Hard cover 1-892065-54-1
        Soft cover 1-892065-55-X

http://www.MeishaMerlin.com

First MM Publishing edition: September 2001

Printed in the United States of America
0 9 8 7 6 5 4 3 2 1

Table of Contents

Author's Note

If this book is your first exposure to the Myth-Adventures of Aahz and Skeeve, there is no reason for you to read this note. Proceed directly to the main body of the work and enjoy.

If, however, you have been following this series for some time, some explanations are in order. Specifically, as to why you are now holding this volume instead of the long-awaited, long-promised episode titled *Something M.Y.T.H. Inc.*

As was noted in Author's Note of the previous volume, *Sweet Myth-tery of Life* (which was also late in being written), I have been going through some difficult times in my life. Since that volume was released in 1994, most of those difficulties revolved around a five-to-six-year death duel with the IRS over back taxes. The less said about that, the better.

When that matter was resolved in April of 2000, I re-applied myself to writing the two overdue MYTH novels, only to find myself in a dilemma. The first problem was that it had been over seven years since I had written Aahz and Skeeve, and it was extremely difficult after that long a hiatus to recapture the style and rhythm of the narration and dialogue that had made the series unique. To complicate things, the story I was attempting to convey, *Something M.Y.T.H. Inc.*, was the most complex tale I had attempted in the MYTH series, as it not only involves multiple viewpoints, but also occurs simultaneously with events contained in *Sweet Myth-tery of Life.*

After nearly half a year of wrestling with these difficulties, a friend of mine made a suggestion. Specifically, why not write another, simpler story first...something from Skeeve's earlier days with Aahz. That would enable me to relearn the MYTH writing style, after which I could tackle the more convoluted story of *Something M.Y.T.H. Inc.*

The result is the volume you are currently holding. Sequentially, it occurs between volumes three—*Myth-Direction*—and four—*Hit or Myth*. (They will be republished in the combined omnibus *Myth Adventures Two* in February 2002 from Meisha Merlin Publishing, Inc.) If the plan holds, *Something M.Y.T.H. Inc.* will follow it VERY shortly.

As always, thank you for your loyalty and patience.

Robert Lynn Asprin
February 2001

Myth-ion Improbable

by

Robert

Lynn

Asprin

Chapter One

"Here we go again!"
C-3PO

When my teacher/mentor Aahz grumbles or rants about my being stupid or having done something stupid, I make a big show of being apologetic, but it really doesn't bother me all that much. I figure it goes with the territory and is part of the price of learning magik.

I mean, first of all, there's the point that Aahz is older than I am and has been around more. A *lot* more. He's an experienced dimension traveler, or 'demon' for short, and compared to his knowledge and experience I really *am* stupid and naive.

Then, too, the dimension he hails from, Perv, is noted for its short-tempered, hostile inhabitants. Other dimension travelers tend to avoid Perv whenever possible, and give the green, scaly Pervects a wide berth when encountering them in other dimensions.

To cap it all off, while he was once an accomplished magician himself, Aahz lost his powers when we met (See *Another Fine Myth*). Watching me fumble and stutter while learning what are, to him, some of the simplest, most rudimentary spells, all the while being aware that, at least for the time being, he's dependent on me in the magik department, is bound to make him a bit testy from time to time.

I can understand and accept it when I do something he thinks is stupid. When I do something that, in hindsight, I *think* is stupid...that's another matter entirely.

We were ensconced in the Royal Palace of the Kingdom of Possiltum, enjoying my cushy position as the Royal Court Magician, a job that Aahz had coached me through the auditions for. That is, Aahz was enjoying it. For him it was comfortable surroundings and a steady, generous salary. For me, it was living in constant close contact with a grouchy demon who seemed determined that I practice my magik lessons night and day.

Needless to say, this gets boring after a while. The few adventures I had been on since I had apprenticed myself to Aahz had whetted my appetite for travel, and I was eager for more. Unfortunately, Aahz steadfastly refused to even start teaching me how to dimension-travel on my own, saying it was far too dangerous for someone with my meager magikal abilities.

That's when I decided to try something really stupid. I decided to try to outwit Aahz and trick him into taking me dimension traveling again.

An item had come to hand that I thought might be just the ticket, so one afternoon when he seemed a bit bored himself, I sprang it on him.

"Aahz," I said, holding out a folded piece of parchment to him, "I think you should take a look at this."

Aahz glared at the paper in my hand as if it might bite him. And when someone from Perv glares, it is really something to see.

"And just what is that?"

"It looks like a map." I shrugged.

Actually, I knew it was a map. While Tanda and I had been jumping dimensions, shopping for a birthday present for Aahz, I had been offered this map by a beggar on a street corner. Since Tanda had been, at that moment, off talking to some sort of businessmen of that dimension, I had bought the map for a few coins, thinking it would be a fun small gift. I had stuck the map in my belt pouch, and then proceeded to forget about it because of all the problems with the Big Game three dimensions later. Actually, forgetting about the map was entirely understandable, since Tanda ended up captured and our main focus was on freeing her. And the only way we could free her was by winning the game. So forgetting the map was reasonable. I had had enough on my mind.

But today, while searching through my pouch for something else, I found the map. While I honestly didn't know what it was, I thought it might be what I needed to bait Aahz into taking me dimension traveling again.

Aahz still wasn't about to touch the parchment. He motioned to the fire.

"Throw it in there and then get back to your practice."

"I'm done with my practice," I said.

"You're never done with your practice."

I ignored him and pushed on.

"Besides, I paid good coins for this map."

That was my trump card. If there's anything Aahz hates, it's wasting money. He got angry with me every time my dragon, Gleep, tore up something while playing, and the cost of repairs were taken from my wages. When it came to my money, Aahz was in complete control. And by the way he talked, we were always broke and about to go hungry.

"A scam, I'm sure," Aahz said, turning away. "Just like you to waste money."

I frowned. This was going to be harder than I thought. Normally, if there was any chance of making money at anything, he jumped at it.

Then it dawned on me I hadn't told him what the map led to.

"Aahz," I said to his back.

He didn't move. Instead he just kept staring out the window at the courtyard.

"Aahz, you might really want to look at this. It's a map to a creature called a cow."

"So?" Aahz said, shaking his head. "Remember the last time we were at the Bazaar at Deva? Where do you think that steak you ate came from?"

I stared at him. I had no idea steaks came from creatures called cows. I had just assumed they came from creatures called steaks. Trout came from trout, salmon came from salmon, and duck came from duck. It was logical. Besides, there were no cows in this dimension. At least, none that I had ever met.

"Well," I said, glancing at the parchment in my hand, "this is a map to a golden cow that lives in a golden palace and gives gold-laced milk."

Aahz slowly turned to stare at me, his eyes slit as if he were trying to figure out if I was actually joking or not. Then, in two steps, he was in front of me, snatching the map from my grasp.

"So there really is such a golden beast?" I asked while he studied the paper.

He didn't respond, so I stood and watched him stare at the map. The writing on it was odd, actually. It didn't show roads, but more like dimensions, energy points, and vortexes. Most of it I didn't understand, and almost none of the map had any names on it, but there was a massive amount about jumping from dimension to dimension that I didn't understand.

Aahz had told me once there were so many dimensions, no one knew the total number, and it was easy to get lost and never make it back when jumping from dimension to dimension. After my shopping trip with Tanda to thirty or forty different dimensions, I was starting to believe him.

Finally he looked down at me, a frown on his ugly face. And when Aahz frowned, which was a great deal of the time, he looked like an animal snarling. His green skin and bright eyes and sharp teeth could be very intimidating if a person wasn't used to it. Luckily, I was.

"So where exactly did you get this?" He fluttered the parchment in my face as he asked the question.

"Bought it from a man on a street corner," I said. "I think it might have been some beggar."

"What dimension?"

"Not a clue." I shrugged. "One of the many Tanda and I visited. You could ask her."

Aahz frowned even more at that.

"What made you buy it?"

Again I shrugged.

"I honestly don't know. I thought you'd have fun with it for your birthday, and the guy said I was the first traveler he'd seen in a long time who might be able to use it and live to tell the tale."

"Could he see through your disguises?" Aahz asked, staring at me.

I tried to remember back to the day. I had used my standard disguise spell, and on that dimension, the spell had not been hard. Most of the residents stood four feet tall, and had two feet. Compared to disguising Tanda and me as slugs on one of the previous dimensions, that had been easy. But the beggar had clearly picked me out of a crowd, and he seemed out of place among the short people, being almost five feet tall.

I looked at Aahz and nodded.

"Maybe. But I don't know how he could have."

Aahz waved his hand in disgust.

"Apprentice, there are a thousand ways, especially with someone so unpracticed as you."

I said nothing. No point in even trying to defend my talents. Aahz always won those conversations by making me try something I couldn't yet do. And that was just about everything when it came to magik. But making disguises *is* my best ability.

Aahz spun around and moved back to the window, keeping the map with him. He stood there, staring out over the courtyard, letting the silence in the room just build and build. And if there was one thing I hated more than anything, it was the sound of someone thinking, without telling me what they were thinking about.

"So, is there such a golden cow?" I asked, moving over and standing beside him in the big window so he couldn't ignore me.

In the courtyard below the window, Gleep was running in circles chasing his tail. Thank heavens he wasn't near anything, because when a dragon started chasing his tail, things got knocked down, trampled, and just flat destroyed. Especially when it was a *young* dragon.

What was even more amazing was that Aahz didn't seem to be noticing what Gleep was doing. Clearly the map meant something to him.

"The golden cow?" I asked again, "Is it real?"

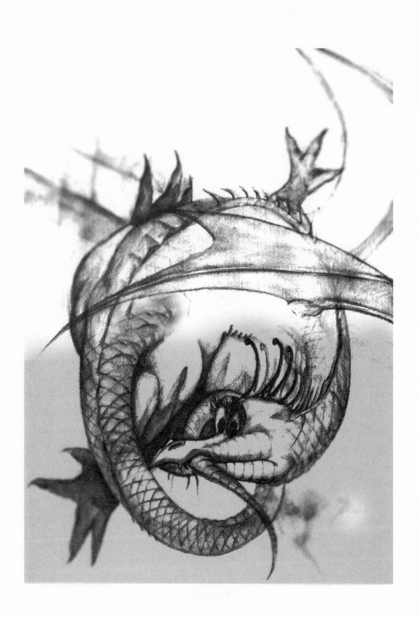

Aahz slowly turned and looked at me.

"A myth. There are a lot of them in the different dimensions."

"You're kidding! You mean there is more than one golden-milk-giving-cow myth?" Considering that I had never heard of a cow before today, I found that a little hard to imagine. I'm not sure exactly why I thought even one golden cow was easy to imagine, but dozens of them were just too much. Maybe there was an entire dimension with a race of them.

Aahz sighed. When he sighed like that, it usually meant I was being extra stupid or dense.

"Every tenth dimension has a myth about an animal or person doing something with gold. One has a goose laying golden eggs, another has a fish touching things and turning them to gold, another has a duck with golden feathers."

"One heavy bird," I said, trying to imagine the duck covered in gold.

Aahz sighed again.

"The feathers become gold when they fall off."

"Got you," I said. "You ever been near or seen one of these golden animals?"

Aahz laughed, his demon-sound shaking the room.

"If I had, would I be here, in this dump of a palace, with an apprentice as stupid as you?"

I had to admit he had a good point, but I didn't really want to agree with him.

"So that is a sham map," I said.

"Most likely," Aahz said, staring out at the courtyard where Gleep had now managed to catch his tail. He bit it so hard, the poor dragon jumped and looked around, startled. Gleep was smart in many ways, but not about his own tail.

I glanced over at Aahz. When he said 'most likely,' and didn't look at me, it meant he thought there might be a slight chance the map was real.

"Why only most likely?" I asked.

"Because," Aahz said, "I saw a golden deer-dropping once."

"Deer dropping?" Again I had no idea what he meant.

"Deer poop," Aahz said, his voice showing he was getting very tired of my stupid questions. "Deer turds. Deer crap. Deer excrement. One dimension has a myth about a deer that drops gold. I saw one of the droppings. And…"

He stopped, still not looking at me. In all the time we had been together, I had never seen him like this before.

"And what?" I asked.

"And I saw part of a solid-gold elk antler at the Bazaar at Deva."

I was stunned. A deer that pooped gold and an elk that had golden antlers.

"So the map might actually be real?"

"I doubt it," Aahz said, glancing at it.

"But you don't know for sure, do you?"

He shook his head.

"Not for sure."

"So we're going to check it out?"

He looked down at the map in his hand, then folded it and stuffed it in his pocket.

"I'll be back in an hour."

He pulled out the D-Hopper and twisted it to a setting. Back before he met me and lost his powers, he used to be able to jump through the dimensions without the use of a D-Hopper. Now he needed the help and he hated it.

"Wait!" I shouted. "You can't go looking for it without me."

"I'm not," Aahz said. "And get that dragon of yours under control before he breaks something again and we have to pay for it. Be ready to go. One hour. And the dragon doesn't come with us."

With that Aahz was gone, vanished off to another dimension with a faint BAMF.

By the time Aahz got back I had Gleep in his stall in the stables and had arranged for someone to feed and walk him until I returned from wherever we were going.

I was standing near the foot of the bed in my room when suddenly the air next to me sort of went BAMF again. Not real loud, but startling when it happened two feet from you. I jumped. Aahz was back, and he had my favorite demon in the entire universe of demons with him.

"Tananda!" I shouted, stepping toward the beautiful creature with the long green hair and a body that, with a deep breath, could stop a parade.

"Skeeve!" she shouted back, laughing.

Then she pulled me into a hug that I hoped would never, ever stop. Now, granted, it had only been a month since I had last seen her, drunk as a skunk at Aahz's birthday party. But every time I saw her I figured it was a great excuse for a very long hug. And she sure didn't seem to mind, either.

Tanda was a former assassin and member of the guild. I wasn't sure what she did now besides shop and go on adventures. What's more, I didn't really want to know. We were friends, and that was enough for me.

Aahz cleared his throat after far too short a time in her wonderful hug. He did seem to mind that she didn't mind. Oh, well. I still believed she liked me better than him, and that was all that mattered.

She pushed me back and looked at me sternly, her wonderful eyes glaring at me with mock anger.

"Why didn't you tell me you had bought a treasure map?"

"Actually, I was going to when we stopped for the night," I said with a shrug, "but then the game and you getting captured and everything sort of pushed the map out of my mind."

"So do you remember how many dimensions before Jahk you bought it?" she asked.

I knew exactly how many, since I had done the disguises in every dimension on the trip. "Three," I said.

"You're absolutely sure?" Aahz asked, his golden eyes staring at me like they were about to shoot daggers.

I held up my hand.

"Jahk, the dimension with the Big Game."

I pointed at my thumb.

Tanda nodded and Aahz just glared, his expression of annoyance making me take my time.

"Counting backwards," I said, pointing at my index finger, "the dimension before that was where we had to look like a form of a three-nosed pig."

I wiggled my index finger at both of them.

Tanda nodded. "Yeah, fun place."

"Not really," I said.

Aahz's glare got deeper, so I went on.

"Before that was the dimension where we had to be eight feet tall and have three legs." I pointed at my middle finger.

Tanda laughed. "That was a fun dimension, too. Wasn't it?"

It hadn't been, since walking on three legs is something that is a factor harder than trying to fly by flapping your arms and jumping off a cliff. But I ignored her this time and went on.

I pointed to my next finger.

"Dimension where we had to be four feet tall and where I bought the map." I held up the three fingers. "That many in front of the game dimension."

I wanted to add that I could go over them again if Aahz wanted, but he was clearly not happy with me, so I didn't offer.

Tanda smiled. "I thought so. Mini."

"So what's so special about that dimension?" I asked.

It hadn't seemed like much to me, although Tanda had not wanted to stay there long on our shopping trip.

"Actually," Aahz said, "it makes this map more likely to be real."

"Almost certain." Tanda laughed.

"You're kidding?" I asked. "You really think there is a golden cow out there?"

"I didn't say that," Aahz said. "I just said the *map* was likely to be real."

I frowned and Tanda laughed.

"Mini is populated by Minikins, who have this awful power of never telling a lie about anything. They do not do well at the Bazaar at Deva, for obvious reasons."

"But what happens if the guy who sold it to me wasn't a Minikin?"

"If he had been there for more than a day, he had to tell the truth about the map as well. That's why we got out of there so fast. Truth is not a good influence when you are shopping."

At that I had no firsthand knowledge, but I figured Tanda was the expert.

"Come on," she said to Aahz. "Dig out the map. We're wasting time. Let's do this."

"Why do I have a bad feeling about this?" Aahz asked as he pulled out the parchment, unfolded it, and put it on the bed so all three of us could look at it.

I had no idea what I was looking at, but Tanda seemed to. She pointed at the upper left corner.

"That's Minikins' Dimension."

Even I knew that, since it was labeled Mini.

"So we start there?"

Aahz nodded. So did Tanda, for which I was grateful. If they both agreed, at least we had something solid.

Tanda ran her finger along the only line leading from Minikin. It ended at a dot that was labeled Vortex #1. She studied that for a moment, then glanced at Aahz.

"You have any idea what that means? Or where it's at?"

"Not a clue," he said.

Now I was stunned. It wasn't often that my mentor admitted he didn't know something. In fact, I couldn't remember the last time that it had happened, if ever. I wanted to point that out to him, but this just didn't seem to be the right time, so I went back to studying the map.

I could see that on the map Vortex #1 had six lines leading off to six unlabeled points on the paper. And lines led off of each of those points to other vortex dots. There were seven more vortexes listed, and a big "x" marking the cow in the lower right corner of the map. Only one line led from Vortex #8 to the cow.

It was clear that there was no straight line from Mini to the cow. And no right path. From the looks of it, we could go any of a dozen different ways, through different points labeled vortexes, taking different lines. If nothing else, this was going to be an interesting puzzle.

Aahz had told me that dimension-hopping was dangerous because a person could hop to an unknown dimension and never get back. I wondered now how safe it was going to be following a map through some of these dimensions, especially when even the map was confusing.

"Well," Tanda said, turning to Aahz. "It looks like we're going to need some more help if we're going to find this golden beast."

Aahz looked at her and then slowly shook his head.

"You can't be thinking what I think you're thinking."

"I'm thinking it," she said.

"No!" Aahz said, his voice firm. I knew for a fact that when he said no like that there was no changing his mind.

"Yes," Tanda said, smiling at him with a smile that could melt a belt-buckle right off a guy's pants. She reached up and touched one of the green scales on his cheek.

"No," Aahz said, but this time it wasn't as firm. Not even a Pervect could stand up against Tanda's charms.

"Yes," she said, turning the smile up one more notch and stroking Aahz's green neck just below his ear.

I was glad she wasn't doing that to me. As it was, just watching I was almost a puddle on the floor. And I didn't even know what they were arguing about.

Aahz wasn't faring much better. He shook his head, then said, "It's a mistake."

"How else are we going to find what dimension to jump to from Minikin?"

She stroked his cheek and then moved right up against him.

No sentient male being could have withstood that attack. Aahz didn't.

I was sweating hard just watching. Much more and I would need to change into one of my clean shirts.

"All right," he said, his voice so soft I could almost not hear it. "But trust me, this is a mistake."

"Oh, we're not showing anyone the map," Tanda said, moving away from Aahz and turning down her convincing body language and smile to a normal level.

Both Aahz and I took a deep breath.

"Then why?" Aahz asked.

"We're just going to find out what, or where a vortex is," Tanda said.

I couldn't stand it any longer.

"Would someone please tell me what this is all about?"

"No," Aahz said.

He picked up the map, then took me by the arm and stepped over beside Tanda. A moment later we were in the Bazaar at Deva.

Chapter Two

"How bazaar!"
RIPLEY

The Bazaar at Deva was like no other place in the universe, or at least that's what Aahz kept telling me. And from my few times in the Bazaar, and what little of the different dimensions I had seen, I was beginning to agree with him.

The Deevels, the residents of Deva, were known as the best traders and negotiators. Now, granted, Aahz, as a Pervect, could be tight with a penny, but as Aahz had warned, a Deevel could trade you out of the penny and the pocket you kept it in, and leave you naked and thinking you were better off for the deal.

The Bazaar was the logical extension of that ability. They had set up the trading capital of all the dimensions, a bazaar that now stretched seemingly forever. Demons, which was a catchphrase for Dimension Travelers, were allowed to set up booths and try to make a living doing whatever it was they did best.

I don't think anyone really knew how far the Bazaar extended, since the tents and booths seemed to always be changing and moving. When I asked how long Aahz thought it would take me to walk across the Bazaar, he said if I was lucky, only five or six months, but he doubted I would make it alive.

It seems that the Bazaar at Deva was also a very dangerous place, which was why I was doing my best to keep up with Tananda and Aahz as they headed through the crowds. I had no idea why this area was so jammed with Demons. It smelled like someone was boiling old shoes, and most of the demons in this area were covered in white and red scales that flaked at the slightest touch. And in my hurry I was bumping into a lot of them. By the time we came to a stop in front of a blank-looking tent with the flap closed, I was sweating like it was a hot summer day, and scales were stuck all over me.

"Might want to brush those off," Aahz said, glancing at me and shaking his head.

Neither he or Tanda seemed to have any on them at all. I had no idea how they had managed that and still moved so fast.

"Why?" I asked, half-heartedly pushing the white and red scales off my sleeve.

"They're acid," Tanda said, reaching over and flicking a scale off my forehead with a polished nail.

I picked up the speed of my brushing, working at getting every one of the hundreds of scales stuck to me.

Tanda and Aahz just laughed.

"Little help with the back?" I asked, shaking my entire body as hard as I could.

Tanda laughed even harder as I turned around and her hands worked over my shoulders, down my back, and across my rear. Any other circumstances I would have enjoyed the feel, but standing in the middle of a crowd with acid scales all over me sort of deflated any thoughts of enjoyment.

Aahz just stood and shook his head, staring at the tent, until I was finished and Tanda had inspected my hair and neck and other areas for a stray scale. I didn't know that we had both missed one in my left shoe until I looked down and saw that my shoe was smoking. It was one of my best pairs, too.

As I kicked off the shoe and emptied the acid scale onto the ground, Aahz looked at me and bared his teeth in a grin.

"Just count your blessings it didn't go down your pants."

I looked at the hole the scale had burnt into my shoe and shuddered.

"Want me to check you to make sure?" Tanda asked, smiling.

"Thanks," I said, putting my shoe back on. "Maybe later."

"I still don't like this idea," Aahz said, turning to stare at the tent, which was clearly why we were on Deva.

Tanda shrugged. "Neither do I, but we don't have much of a choice, do we? You know anyone who might know what or where a vortex is?"

Aahz shook his head, obviously trying to think of someone.

"I just don't like the price we're going to pay."

"It doesn't have to be that bad," she said.

Aahz said nothing.

I finished one more last check for scales and glanced at the tent we were standing in front of. There was no sign, no indication that anyone was even in it. The crowd in the street seemed to give it a wide berth as well.

"I just wish I knew what we were walking into," I said. "A little hint would be nice."

"You're staying out here," Aahz said.

I glanced around at the flowing crowds of white-and-red-scaled acid demons and shook my head. "Not a chance."

"We need to stick together," Tanda said, taking my side. "We may have to move quickly."

"That doesn't sound good," I said.

Aahz made his disgusted noise, then looked me right in the eyes.

"Not a word comes from your mouth in there. Understand?"

"Sure," I said, making a motion across my mouth that I had sealed it.

"Here," Tanda said, smiling at me. "Let me help you with that."

She put her wonderful hand against my mouth. The smell of her skin was that of distant flowers; her touch was soft. She ran her hand along my mouth as I had done, then patted my shoulder.

"That was—"

My mouth wouldn't open!

I tried again.

The words sort of jumbled inside and the only noise that reached my ears was "Thrrrgggg wgggggeeee."

I tried to shout "What did you do?"

What got to my ears was "Wgggggghhh dggggggghhh yggggggghhh dggggggghhh."

My lips were completely glued together. And the harder I tried to force them apart, the more painful it became.

"I didn't know you knew that one," Aahz said to Tanda, completely ignoring my struggle. "I've wanted to use it a hundred times."

She smiled at my mentor. "There are a lot of things you don't know about me."

Well, as far I was concerned, sealing my lips wasn't something I had ever wanted Tanda to do with anything except maybe a kiss. I tried to tell her so, but again nothing sounded like a word.

"Let's do this," Aahz said, nodding in satisfaction at my condition, then stepping toward the tent.

"Don't worry," Tanda said, smiling at my struggle as she took my arm and followed Aahz. "It's just temporary. Trust me, it's for your own good. And ours as well."

Not for the first time, it occurred to me that for someone who claimed not to have enough magikal talent to be a magician, Tanda occasionally displayed a lot more knowledge and skill than I had as the Royal Magician of Possiltum.

At the tent flap Aahz didn't even hesitate or knock, if knocking was possible on a big tent. He just stepped inside and Tanda led me right behind him.

The place was huge.

No, huge didn't describe it. On either side of us the tent seemed to fade off into the distance. This was the first time I had seen one of the Bazaar tents that had bigger insides than outsides. Aahz had mentioned them, but until I stepped into the massive room on the other side of the tent flap, I had no idea that such a thing was really possible. I was going to have to have Aahz teach me the magik involved so I could do that with our rooms back at the palace.

The tent was dimly lit and had a polished marble floor and dark, wooden-looking walls. There was almost no furniture. A simple wooden desk sat on the side of the room facing where we had come in. A massive map of what looked like dimensions filled the wall behind it.

A woman sat at the desk, not looking at us at all. Whatever had Aahz and Tanda so worried about being here wasn't clear on first glance. The room felt odd, but not threatening, besides it being a hundred times larger than the tent holding it.

We all stopped a few feet in front of the desk, with Aahz clearly in the position to do the talking.

The woman looked up at him and smiled. She had deep orange eyes and a pug nose that looked more like a hog's nose than anything like Tanda's. I had never seen a demon like her before.

"Yes?" she asked.

I almost fell over backwards. Her voice was deep, rough, and clearly that of a man. It was with the voice that I actually looked at her. Or him, as I was coming to realize. I had no idea why I had thought he was a woman. His arms and shoulders were built like a man's, and his brownish hair was cut short. Yet I had sworn, until he spoke, that he was a woman. Just thinking about it was getting me confused.

Aahz got right to the point.

"We are looking for directions to a dimension called Vortex."

The man who sort of looked like a woman smiled at Aahz.

Now he was back to being a woman again. And his pig nose had vanished, leaving a wonderful pointed nose and red lips. And as I watched her face shifted slowly. The transformation was amazing. Her eyes changed color, from orange to blue, her skin darkened, her cheeks rose, and her hair grew to her shoulders.

"How the—" I started to ask how she changed like that, but my sealed lips stopped me cold. Aahz and Tanda said nothing. Clearly they had expected to meet a shape-shifting demon in here. It was as if she were constantly working through disguise spells. Interesting trick, that was for sure.

"Well," she said, her voice now soft and rich and alluring, "which Vortex are you looking for?"

Aahz seemed to struggle for a moment with the answer. I wanted to blurt out that we needed the first eight of them, but luckily my mouth was glued shut. I had no idea why I wanted to blurt that out.

"Vortexes #1 through #8," Aahz said.

The demon behind the desk was slowly shifting to look like a stone statue, her clothes vanishing into her body as she changed into a rock-like demon with scales for skin and arms as thick as trees. I also noticed that the chair it was on changed with the size of the creature at the moment. More than likely the chair was part of its body as well.

"What is the nature of your reason for wanting the location of these places?" the shifting creature asked, its voice rumbling like thunder inside the massive room.

Again Aahz struggled with the answer. I had no doubt in my mind I wanted to blurt out that we had a treasure map. Something about this creature clearly forced demons standing in front of it to tell the truth. Now I was grateful that Tanda had closed my mouth. I had no idea how they were keeping quiet. What I was feeling was clearly very powerful magik or mind control.

"We are searching for a treasure," Aahz said, his words measured and slow, "and our path leads us through the Vortex dimensions, starting with Vortex #1."

"Logical," the creature said as it shifted toward a pig-body shape.

"The price is 10% of your find."

I could see the anger growing in Aahz's body, his green scales stiff on his neck. Giving away anything to do with money was beyond something Aahz could do without undue stress.

Tanda put her hand on his arm and stepped forward.

"Your price is high for simple directions. We will give you 5% of anything we acquire on this venture, no matter what the value. Otherwise we will look elsewhere for help."

The creature now looked like a quatra-piggy, a type of demon I had seen in the street on an earlier trip here. But that body was quickly changing to a new shape.

"You will not find help elsewhere," the shifting demon said. "But your offer is fair and I will accept. I assume you need to go to Vortex #1 first?"

"Yes," both Aahz and Tanda said at the same time.

The creature, now shifting back into a beautiful woman again, nodded. "That can be arranged."

She looked at Aahz and Tanda with a serious look. Her voice was firm and very solid. "Since I have a financial stake now in what you are attempting, I must warn you that a Vortex dimension is not a place to take lightly. It is a very dangerous, and sometimes tempting, place. It will be very easy to miss your path and become lost."

Then she looked at me, her beautiful blue eyes boring into my heart. In my best dreams I would remember what this creature looked like forever. She had transformed into the most striking female I could have ever imagined. Every part of my body wanted to move to her, to touch her, to never leave her.

Her gaze seemed to bore deeper and deeper into me as my legs got weak and my stomach did flip-flops. I desperately wanted my lips to be free to tell her how much I loved her.

"You must take care of your friends," she said, her wonderful voice melting every thought I had. "Understand?"

I managed to nod.

"Good," she said, winking at me. "I will know if you succeed or fail. Good luck to you."

With that the tent and the beautiful woman were gone.

Around us a wind whipped over the plains, driving dirt and dust into my face.

"Vortex #1," Aahz shouted over the blowing wind.

"Here we go," Tanda shouted back.

I just wish someone had warned me we were jumping dimensions.

"Pgghhhhh ugghhhhh mgggghhhh mggghhhh" was all I managed to say.

The dust blew around my head, reducing visibility to near zero. The changing demon back in the big tent on Deva had said the Vortex dimensions were dangerous and full of temptations. The only temptation I had about this place was an instant desire to go home.

"This way! Hurry!"

Tananda motioned that we should follow her. Since there
was nothing to be seen but swirling dust, I figured I had nothing to lose.

It seemed that my closed-lip problem was as temporary as
Tanda had promised it would be. By the time she had led us a
hundred staggering paces through the storm to what looked to
be an old log cabin, my lips were again free.

The old cabin that Tanda had led us to had been made of
cut-together logs and had to be a hundred years old. She shoved
the door open and we stomped inside. Wind blew in through
at least a hundred cracks in the walls and the only things that
now lived in the place was rodents.

"What was the big rush?" Aahz said, brushing dust from
his clothes after shoving the door closed.

"Didn't you see it?" Tanda said. "There was something
moving out there. Moving toward us."

"I must have missed it," Aahz said, and looked at me.

All I could do was shake my head and shrug. I hadn't seen
anything either, but Tanda seemed a bit spooked.

I got a pretty decent fire in the middle of the dirt floor,
using nothing but my mind and a bunch of wood, as Tanda
put a containment field around the room to keep out the wind.

As it turned out, both Tanda and Aahz had expected something to happen when we went into that tent. They were pretty
much prepared. I just wish they had warned *me* to get ready.

After I finished the fire, Tanda hung a translation pendant
around my neck, then another around Aahz's neck, just in case
we ran into someone we couldn't understand when we jumped
from here.

"So," I said, holding my hands out to warm them over the
fire, "could you please explain just what happened, who the
shifting demon was, how we got here, and where 'here' is?"

"You know," Aahz said to Tanda, ignoring me, "I think I
liked him better with his mouth sealed."

"Sealing a guy's lips isn't a nice thing to do," I said. Then
I thought back to what I had wanted to say while in the tent
and luckily hadn't been able to. "But I understand why you
did it. A compulsion spell, right?"

Aahz now looked at me with a shocked expression as Tanda laughed.

"I think your apprentice is starting to learn," she said, smiling at Aahz. "Might as well answer his questions."

Aahz just sighed and sat down on the floor.

"The tent we went into was a Shifter's tent. The person we had talked to was a Shifter. The Shifter moved us here, and my guess is this wonderful place is the Vortex #1 dimension."

I had to admit that he had answered my questions, but not very well.

"So why were you so reluctant to go see a Shifter for help?"

Tanda laughed at that as she too sat down on the floor.

"It wasn't just Aahz. I didn't want to either, but we had no choice, if we really were going to follow the map."

"Why?"

"Because," Aahz said, "Shifters have made it their business to know where dimensions are. Remember I told you that when jumping to a dimension you need to have a clear image of that dimension in mind, as well as a solid place in the dimension?"

I nodded. Every time I asked Aahz to start teaching me how to dimension-hop he brought that problem up.

"I might be able to jump to a few hundred," Aahz said, "if I had my powers back and I was close enough to them. Maybe between Tanda and me we could find three or four hundred. With a really expensive D-Hopper we might find another few hundred on top of that. But there are thousands and thousands of dimensions. Maybe even millions, for all I know. The Shifters are the travel agents of dimensions."

"What's a travel agent?"

I looked at Tanda, then at Aahz. Both were just shaking their heads.

"Never mind," Aahz said, waving the question away with his hand. Every time he did that, I knew he considered the question too stupid for an answer.

"So they charge for the information and the jump," I said, going on. "Sounds reasonable to me."

"Well, it is and it isn't," Tanda said. "No one knows where the Shifters come from. They are masters of disguise, and if you try to double-cross them you will disappear, never to be seen again."

"More than likely off to some deadly dimension," Aahz said, shaking his head.

"So we make sure they get their five percent of the golden cow if we find it."

That seemed logical enough to me.

"I hope that's all it will take," Aahz said.

Tanda just nodded.

I didn't like that at all. Disappearing was not something I considered in my possible future. I had plans. Better, bigger plans. Yet now I was risking my life chasing a cow. Not smart at all as far as I was concerned. I tried to think about something else besides a future where someone made me vanish.

"How do the Shifters keep changing like that one did?"

"Disguise spells, maybe. I don't know. " Tanda shrugged. "I've never seen one really stay the same for very long."

I considered myself good at disguises, but I was a long way from being able to do what that Shifter had been doing. Which meant that if they were that good, it was possible that one of the shifters was with us right now, disguised as something around the room.

The thought almost made me jump. I glanced around, trying to see anything odd about the old log cabin. There was nothing but a dirt-littered floor and old logs. Yet I now had a feeling we were being watched.

"So let's see if we can figure out where we are and how to take the next step," Tanda said, scooting over beside Aahz.

I walked once around the small room, then moved over to where Aahz had pulled out the map and spread it on the floor.

"Would you look at that?" Tanda said, pointing.

I saw instantly what she was talking about. The map had changed. I studied what was there now, comparing it to what had been there before. Now the lines from Vortex #1 were

different, and the points at the end of each were labeled. And
the upper corner of the map had Deva listed, with a direct line
from Deva to Vortex #1.

"Amazing," Aahz said, his voice just a whisper. "A true
treasure map."

"How did it do that?" I asked.

Aahz laughed.

"Just as everything is done," he said. "Magik."

"It's a magik map, a true treasure map of the dimensions,"
Tanda said. "I've only heard of such things."

She reached over and gave me a big hug, something I was
more than willing to continue as long as she wanted it to.
Finally, far too quickly, she let go and looked at me.

"This was a great purchase on your part."

I shrugged. "Not unless it leads somewhere."

"True," Aahz said, not looking up from the map.

I went back to studying the map as well. As far as I was
concerned, it was just lines and points and a few names. I
couldn't use it to find my way back to where we had appeared
here on Vortex #1, let alone to jump dimensions.

"So the map changes. What does that mean?"

Tanda pointed at the point labeled Vortex #1.

"Thanks to the Shifter, we're here. From this point we
have five choices of dimension jumps."

She pointed to the five names the lines lead to from this
place. "The one called Bumppp looks the most promising."

Aahz nodded. "And the straightest line through the map
as well."

"You know this Bumppp world?" I asked. "Or any of
those places?"

She slowly shook her head.

"Aahz?"

"No, I don't."

I looked at him, then at Tanda, remembering what Aahz
had told me about dimension hopping. You had to know exactly where you were going, or you couldn't jump.

"So we're stuck here?" I asked. "That's the end of the
trip?"

"No," Aahz said, reaching into his belt pouch and pulling out a D-Hopper.

He quickly scrolled through the listing of dimensions on the Hopper, checking them with the names on the map. Finally, he sighed and put it back.

And with that sigh I knew we were done. The five possible places we could jump to from this place was not on the D-Hopper either.

"Damn," Tanda said. "I was afraid this might happen."

She pushed herself to her feet and brushed off her pants.

"I hate this," Aahz said, standing. He carefully folded the map and put it in his belt pouch.

"What are we doing now?"

Tanda motioned that I should come closer. Then she reached up, and before I could stop her, she sealed my lips again.

"Sorry," she said. "Can't take the chance."

I tried to object, but the only thing that came out was "Wggghhh."

This was getting old. Too much more of this kind of treatment and my lips were going to be sore for a week.

A moment later, without a warning from either Tanda or Aahz, we were back standing in front of the Shifter in the big tent.

Chapter Three

"There's no such thing as a free ride."
M.T.A.

"Ten percent for your solution," the Shifter said, its voice deep and strong as it studied Tanda and scratched what seemed to be part of its neck.

I stared at it, not really looking at what it was at the moment, but more studying how it was changing constantly. It was as if there was always a part of it moving, morphing into the next character. The hair shifted, the skin changed, the arms lengthened, nothing really staying complete for more than a few seconds before starting to change into the next shape or color. Its voice, its chair, its eyes all changed as well. That really impressed me. When I did a disguise spell, I could do clothing and size and shape, but never the quality of the eyes. From this Shifter's eyes it looked as if it was actually fifty or a hundred different beings all melding together. For all I knew, it was. I wanted to ask it how it did what it did, but then remembered my lips were again sealed.

"Ten percent!" Aahz said through his teeth, his voice barely under control.

"On top of the first five percent, bringing the total to fifteen percent."

I thought I could see a blood vessel in Aahz's neck trying to break out from under the green scales. Any moment Tanda was going to have to seal his mouth as well, from the looks of it. I wanted to tell the Shifter how greedy it was being, but luckily I couldn't.

"No," Tanda said. "We will give you another five percent, and five percent more for each time we require your help in this journey, but not one bit above that."

The Shifter had become a tall creature with a very thin face and hundreds of tiny teeth crammed into a very ugly mouth. And at that moment the mouth smiled, or at least did something I thought was a smile.

"Agreed," it said.

Aahz looked like he might have a small fit right there, but somehow he managed to contain himself. I was impressed. It wasn't often that large percentages of a possible fortune were taken from him and he didn't destroy something. Aahz and money were not easily parted, and if we did find this golden cow, there was no doubt in my mind that Aahz would not want to part with much of the golden milk. But now he would have no choice, for at least ten percent of the find.

And I had no doubt we were going to be back here a number more times before this little venture was over.

"What is your destination now?" it asked.

"Bumppp," Tanda said.

For a moment the creature hesitated, and I thought I saw the morphing hesitate as well. Then it said, almost sadly, "Very well."

A moment later we ended up in the middle of a wide meadow filled with thick plants and orange flowers. The sky overhead was a faint blue and pink. Dark-green trees surrounded the meadow, and in the distance there were pink mountains. I had been ready to use my disguise spell on us to protect us from any storm, but the air was warm and humid, just the way I liked it.

Actually, all in all, this was one of the most beautiful dimensions I had visited. I wondered what kind of lucky people lived here.

Tanda turned a full circle, her sharp eyes taking in things I knew I didn't see.

"Ten percent?" Aahz said, his teeth still grinding.

Tanda put her finger to her mouth for Aahz to be silent. I instantly started searching the tree-line for any sign of danger. There was nothing that I could see. No natives with weapons, no crouching tigers, no charging bears.

Nothing.

But clearly from Tanda's actions and the attitude and hesitation of the Shifter, this wasn't a friendly place. Beautiful, but not friendly.

"The map," she whispered to Aahz. "Quickly."

Then she motioned that we should all crouch down.

The weeds and flowers covering the meadow were no more than knee-high and would give us no cover at all. They smelled like my dragon when he got wet.

I figured we should move to the edge of the trees. At least there we might have a fighting chance if something came at us. But Tanda was the ex-assassin among us. She knew what she was doing. Or at least I hoped she did.

Aahz opened the map and laid it out carefully on top of the weeds. It was clear instantly that the map had again changed. Bumppp, the dimension we were in, showed clearly, with only one path leading from this world toward the dream of our very own golden cow. And that path led to Vortex #4.

Not #2, as I would have expected, or even #3, but #4.

Tanda nodded and motioned for Aahz to quickly fold up the parchment and put it away. Then she stood.

I stood right with her, and the moment I did I saw movement. Not just some movement, but all around the edges of the meadow the weeds and flowers were jerking and swaying as if something was running under them at us.

Then a head poked up about a hundred paces from us. A massive snake head that was larger than my head, with yellow, swirling slits for eyes and huge fangs. There was no telling how long the snake's body was, and I really didn't want to wait around and find out.

And then another stuck its head up to the right of the first one. And another and another.

I spun like a dancer. We were surrounded by giant snakes with very nasty-looking fangs. If we didn't do something quickly we were going to end up the main course for lunch.

"Nice place," Aahz said as the moving grass got closer and closer around us.

"Any time now," I tried to suggest, but the only thing that came out of my still sealed mouth was "Aggghhh tgggghhhh nggghhhh."

"What's the matter?" Tanda asked, smiling at me. "Afraid of a little snake?"

I nodded vigorously as another monster snake head popped up not more than fifty paces from us. It looked not only hungry, but angry.

"Yeah," she said, "me, too."

With that we were back in the dust storm on Vortex #1.

"Skeeve!" Aahz yelled as the dust pounded into us.

Before I could even act, Tanda said, "Don't bother."

Then we were back in the Shifter's tent, staring at the creature who now looked just a little too much like the snakes we had just left.

"I am glad for my percentage to see that you have returned," it said.

"I'll bet," Aahz said.

"Vortex #4 please," Tanda said, getting right to business.

"The total is now fifteen percent."

"I understand our agreement," Tanda said before Aahz could say a word. "Vortex #4 please."

The snakelike-shaped Shifter nodded, and again we were whisked through to another dimension.

And right back into the same stupid dust storm.

Okay, I have to admit that when we dimension-hopped back into the dust storm, I was shocked.

Tanda motioned that we should follow her. It took me almost all the way to our destination before I realized where we were. Now granted, I had the excuse that it was blowing heavily. And to me, one dust storm looks just like another. But it wasn't until the old log cabin loomed up out of the dust like a ship in the fog that it dawned on me that we were back in the same place.

Only it wasn't the same place. This was supposed to be Vortex #4, not Vortex #1.

Inside the old building it became clear that we were in a slightly different place. This time, instead of being bare, the inside of the log cabin was filled with branches and some old furniture, and there was no sign of the fire I had built.

"Did you see them this time?" Tanda demanded.

"See what?" Aahz frowned.

"Out there in the storm." she said. "This time I got a good look at them."

"What was it?"

"Dust bunnies. A whole pack of them." She wrapped her arms tightly around herself and shuddered.

Aahz and I looked at each other and shrugged. Again we seemed to be oblivious to whatever it was that was setting Tanda on edge.

By the time I got a new fire going and Tanda had put a containment protection around the cabin to keep the wind out, my lips had unsealed. They were chapped and sore, but at least they were loose.

"So Vortex #4 is a lot like Vortex #1," I said.

"Makes sense," Tanda said. "Otherwise, why give them the same names with only different numbers?"

"Any other dimensions so similar that they could be numbered like this?"

"More than likely," Tanda said, "but I've never seen or heard about any."

"So we paid another five percent to that thief for this?" Aahz said, clearly disgusted. "We could have found this on our own."

I had no idea how he thought we could have done that, but since I didn't know much about dimension-hopping, I said nothing.

"Not likely," Tanda said. "We are a long, long way from Vortex #1. We're farther away in number of dimensions from the Bazaar at Deva than I have ever been before."

"Oh," Aahz said.

"And you know that how?" I asked. "Is there some sort of mileage marker I keep missing in the blink of eye it takes to hop to a new dimension?"

Tanda laughed. "Don't we wish."

"When a person is dimension-hopping," Aahz said, "and they have powers to do it, like Tanda does, you get a sense of how many dimensions away you have jumped. Not precise, but just a sense of distance."

Tanda nodded. "And the farther away in number of dimensions, the harder the jump. And the greater the chance of missing the target and getting lost."

"So that's why you took us back through Vortex #1 from Bumppp?"

"Safer that way," she said.

"And each of our jumps following this map is getting us farther and farther away from home?" I didn't much like the idea of that happening. My job as the Royal Court Magician wasn't much, but at the moment it was better than this place.

"So far," Tanda said. "But this *is* a treasure map we're following. It isn't supposed to be so easy that just anyone could do it."

I didn't like the sound of that, either.

Aahz pulled off his gloves and took out the map, spreading it on the floor so we could all see it by the light of the fire. As expected, the map had changed again. There were now six lines leading from Vortex #4, all to points that now had names. All six lines headed in the general direction of the point marked as the treasure, but none directly. This map wasn't making anything easy, that was for sure.

The names on each dimension this time were stranger than normal. All were combinations of the same five letters. Starting from the left, the names were Et, Cet, Era, Etc, Ete, and Ra.

"You know any of those dimensions?" Aahz asked.

"No," Tanda said. "You?"

"No," Aahz said. "There goes another five percent."

Tanda shrugged. "Can't be helped. I suggest we head for the center one."

"Etc it is, then," I said.

All Aahz did was growl deep inside his throat as he stood and put the map away.

"I hope this means we're going back to Vortex #1 again." I said. "Tell me we're not visiting the snakes again."

"It would be safer if we hit Bumppp again," she said. "No point in taking the chance."

"You can't be serious," I said. Just at the mention of those snakes my stomach clamped up into a knot.

She laughed. "Don't worry. From here I can hit Vortex #1. No snakes needed."

She made sure Aahz was ready, then we hopped.

The dust pounded at me for all of five seconds while Tanda made sure we were there and all right, then she hopped us again right back into the tent of the Shifter.

He was now shaped like a sofa with eyes on the arms and pillows where the ears would be. A massive, orange tongue hung out of the face, forming the seating area. From that moment onward, sitting on a sofa was going to take on a whole new meaning for me.

"We need the Etc dimension," Tanda said.

"Your total is now twenty percent," the creature said, its massive tongue moving as if someone was fluffing the pillows.

"We are aware of that," Tanda said.

The next moment we found ourselves standing on a wide and, mercifully, empty street. Plain-looking wooden buildings framed both sides of the street.

The sky overhead was cloudy and gray, the air was cold and crisp, but at least it wasn't blowing. I was glad I still had our heavy coats and hats on as disguises.

I turned slowly around. There was no doubt there were some strange dimensions in this universe. The road seemed to go off into the distance in both directions from where we were standing, framed by exactly the same types of buildings on both sides, all the same height. Each building had a strange shape to it as well, with two doors, and matching windows. There was no way to tell what was on the other side of the buildings, since it was like we were standing in a canyon.

I had no idea how anyone living in this place found his or her way home. Every building was exactly like the one it butted against, with no numbers or colors or any kind of distinguishing marks.

"Wonder where the people are?" I asked.

"Let's check the map and not wait to find out the answer to that," Aahz said as he headed for the side of the street.

"Yeah," Tanda said as she looked around, clearly on guard. "I don't like the looks of this."

Aahz pulled the map out as he got near the edge of the road and opened it. On the map the dimension we were in was now marked clearly, with only one path leading away from it. Vortex #6 was our next stop. At least we had jumped over Vortex #5 just like we had over #2 and #3.

Tanda glanced at the map and shook her head.

For a moment I thought Aahz was going to wad the thing up and toss it away, but then he folded it and put it back in his jacket.

Suddenly, in the window of the building closest to us, a creature appeared.

"We have company," I said softly.

Tanda and Aahz both looked up as another creature appeared in the window beside the first one.

I glanced around. Every window of every building now had someone standing in it. And every one of them looked exactly alike. Gray suit, gray hair, gray face, two arms. They were all the same shape and same height.

And when one of them moved, every other creature I could see moved the same way.

"This is creeping me out," Tanda said.

The next instant the dust smashed into my face.

"Warning next time," Aahz said.

"This is Vortex #4," she shouted over the wind. "We're hopping again before the bunnies find us."

For an instant there was no dust, then it hit again.

I knew this had to be Vortex #1. I mean, with the dust and all, what else could it be?

Then we were back in the tent with the Shifter. And right at that moment what I really wanted to do more than anything else was just walk out of the tent and forget this entire thing.

"Vortex #6 please," Tanda said to the Shifter, who had lost his couch shape and now looked more like a cross between a cat and a table.

"Twenty-five percent."

Aahz ground his teeth, the sound filling the tent.

"You're making my friend angry by repeating that," I said. Then I realized I had spoken my mind. Tanda hadn't sealed my lips for this visit. Aahz glared at me and I shrugged.

"It is a bargain at twice the price," the Shifter said.

I was about to tell him that dealing with a Deveel was a bargain as well, but Tananda put her hand over my mouth and spoke to the Shifter. "Vortex #6 please. We have agreed to twenty-five percent total to this point."

The Shifter nodded, which looked a lot like a table lifting its leg, then we were back in the dust storm.

It seemed like the same dust, and was as hard to walk in as the last two Vortex dimensions. But as we got near the old cabin, I noticed a very large and very important difference.

This time there was a light in the window.

Someone was home.

Chapter Four

"Don't pick up hitchhikers!"
D. ADAMS

The yellow light coming from the cabin window was like a warning sign. We all stopped about twenty paces short of the door and stared through the blowing dust at the light. I know I was annoyed. After using the cabin in two other dimensions, I was starting to feel like it was an extension of home.

How dare anyone actually live in it?

"Now what do we do?" I shouted to Aahz over the sound of the storm whipping around us.

"Anything else close by?" Aahz asked Tanda.

His green scales on his face were plastered in dust. I knew for a fact he hated being dirty, and after giving away so much of an as-yet-unfound fortune to a travel guide, or agent, or whatever he had called the Shifter, the dust and wind couldn't be helping his mood any.

Tanda shook her head.

"No dust bunnies and nothing else I know of. The Shifter only put directions to this place in my mind on the first hop."

"So we knock," I said over the wind.

Tanda and Aahz seemed to have no other idea, so I slogged through the deep dust to the door and rapped on it.

Tanda moved over to my left and Aahz stayed five steps away in the background, his face covered. If I had to, I would disguise him quickly. His green scales and looks tended to frighten a lot of people.

The door opened suddenly and I found myself facing a girl. She was wearing a long-sleeved shirt, dark pants, and had her hair pulled back off her face. She had a smile that lit up her deep brown eyes and warmed every nerve in my body. I figured her to be about my age. Her face brightened when she saw me.

"You must be Skeeve," she said. "Come on in. My dad said you'd be along eventually."

I stood in the dust, staring at her. In all my life I had never been so surprised at anything anyone said.

She knew my name.

She had been expecting me.

God knew how many dimensions from home and in the middle of a raging dust storm, she had been expecting me!

My first thought was to back slowly away before turning and running into the storm. But my legs remained frozen in place, my mind too stunned to even try to reason out anything.

"Come on," the girl said. "It's windy out there!"

Nothing on me was moving.

Tanda finally pushed me forward and the girl stepped back, holding the door for all of us to go inside.

If I hadn't known this was the same cabin as we had seen in the other dimensions, I would have never have recognized it. Now it had a wooden floor, the cracks in the walls were all filled, and it was warm and comfortable.

There was a table with a bowl of fruit on it, four chairs, and kitchen counter with cabinets on one side of the room. A fire was burning in a baking stove, keeping the cabin comfortable. A bed was against the far wall, with a beautiful blue and gold quilt neatly covering it and a pillow.

The young lady didn't seem to be at all surprised to see Aahz, which worried me even more. Pervects tended to scare people, either by their looks or their reputations.

I finally managed to find the words I needed to ask.

"How do you know me?"

"She knows you?" Aahz asked.

Clearly he had been too far out in the dust storm to hear her over the blowing wind.

The girl laughed and I got even more afraid of her. The laugh was perfect, sort of gentle, yet free and high, like a soft breeze on a summer's afternoon. The exact laugh I would expect from a young lady as beautiful as she was, yet never got, at least from the few I had met.

"I doesn't really know him," she said, again laughing. "At least not in the traditional sense, or any other sense for that matter. Although I must say, I wouldn't mind, if you know what I mean."

I had no idea what she meant. I wanted to ask just how many senses of 'know' there were, but figured I'd wait to do that later.

Aahz snorted and Tanda laughed.

She went on. "My father said I should expect a young, good-looking man named Skeeve to come here. I just assumed you were Skeeve, since you are the first person to visit this place in the two weeks I've been here."

I think I was staring at her, stunned. At least that was how it felt. I didn't know her and I had no idea who her father might be.

She smiled at me and then turned to Tananda.

"You must be the one Skeeve was traveling with before," she said. "Don't worry. I've taken care of the dust bunnies. You know, don't you, that they're completely invisible to guys."

Then she glanced at Aahz and frowned slightly.

"But I don't know you and your connection to this, big guy."

I was so shocked, I couldn't say anything. She had called Aahz 'big guy,' and knew I had traveled with Tanda.

No one said anything.

Clearly Tanda and Aahz were shocked as well. From what Tanda had said, we were a lot of dimensions away from our homes. Yet in the middle of a dust storm, in a strange dimension, we had found someone waiting for us. Someone who knew my name.

"Cat's got your tongues, I see," she said, laughing. She turned around and motioned that we should sit down at the table. "I bet you're getting hungry by now, after all the dimension-hopping you've been doing."

I wanted to ask why she thought a cat had my tongue, and how she knew what we had been doing, then decided against asking that, in exchange for what I thought was a better question.

"Are you a Shifter?"

Again she laughed, the wonderful sound filling the cabin and blending in with the faint crackling of the fire in the oven.

"Not hardly. But my father said you might be getting a little tired of their costs by now. How much of the treasure have you given away so far? Thirty-five percent? Forty percent?"

"Only twenty-five percent," I said.

Then it dawned on me that she knew about the treasure as well. And that we had been negotiating with the Shifters. How much did she know, and how did she know it?

Aahz gave me a stern look and I shrugged. He always thought I talked too much, and clearly this was one of those times he just might be right.

"Wow, you must be a great negotiator," she said, smiling at me.

"Not hardly," Tanda said, moving over and sitting down at the table.

Aahz and I did the same.

"So you know our friend Skeeve here," Tanda said. "Could you please tell us what your name is, and how you know him?"

The girl smiled at me, holding my gaze in her beautiful brown eyes.

"My name is Glenda. My father sold Skeeve the map you are using to search for the golden cow."

Glenda turned back to the counter and opened a cabinet that contained what looked to be a freshly baked loaf of bread.

Tanda glared and me and I just shrugged. I had told her and Aahz everything that had happened when I bought the map. This young lady had been nowhere around That much I was sure of. I would have remembered seeing her.

Now I was even more confused. Why had the guy who sold me the map sent his daughter here to meet us? For what reason?

"So the map was a scam after all," Aahz said, scowling at her, "and you've been waiting here to collect something from us. Is that it?"

Glenda laughed and smiled at Aahz. "The cynic of the group, I see."

Then she smiled at me again.

I smiled right back at her.

"He *does* tend to look at what could go wrong a lot."

"He would make a great lawyer," she said.

I wanted to ask what a lawyer was, but just nodded instead.

She turned to look directly at Aahz.

"No, I assure you that, as far as I know, or *anyone* knows, the map is real."

"So what are you doing here, then?" Tanda asked.

Glenda shrugged. "My father thought you might need some help about now. And when my father told me about Skeeve after he bought the map, I thought he might be cute. I was right."

I think I blushed from the ends of my toes to the top of my head. Luckily the only thing visible to her was my face.

Aahz snorted even louder, an ugly sound that seemed to just hang in the warm cabin like a bad smell.

"Why would your father think we need help?" Tanda asked.

Glenda went back to cutting the fresh bread as she answered. "Because no one has ever made it past this point before, and returned alive."

"Ohhhhh," Aahz said, *"now* I understand. Your father keeps selling the map over and over and your job is to get it back."

"Actually, he's tired of selling it," Glenda said. "And getting it back has never been a problem. He usually just pops in here every spring and takes it off the bodies."

The faint crackling of the fire and the wind against the eaves of the cabin were the only noises. I didn't want to think about the fact that a map I had carried around for a week had been on dead bodies.

"Why does that happen?" Tanda asked, but I noticed that she wasn't really putting as much anger into her voice as before.

Glenda smiled at her. "You're the one with the ability to dimension-hop. You tell me."

Tanda's eyes seemed to fade out for a moment, then she looked up at Glenda and said softly,. "We're too far away from any place I know, including the last place we jumped to."

"Exactly," Glenda said, putting the cut bread on the table in front of us. "The Shifters have done that to six groups of treasure-seekers that my father sold the map to. Vortex #6, this place, is just too far from any known dimension, and any other dimension on the map, for almost anyone but the most traveled dimension-hopper. And until I fixed this cabin up a few weeks ago, there was nothing here but a shell of old logs."

"We would have starved to death," I said.

"Given time, you would have starved, or jumped to some other dimension and gotten lost," Glenda said, pulling out the chair and sitting down beside me. "My father tracked two groups with the map who did that. Both met very ugly ends at the hands of creatures they never should have faced."

My memory of the snakes was clear enough to understand exactly what she was saying.

She took a piece of the wonderful-smelling fresh bread and bit into it, never taking her gaze from mine.

"And your price to rescue us is...?" Aahz asked.

I glanced at him. Typical Aahz, always leading with the pocketbook first.

Glenda smiled at my green-scaled mentor.

"What's your name?" she asked.

"Aahz," he said. "And you haven't answered my question yet."

"I want to go with you," she said. "And for helping you find the golden cow and getting us all back to a dimension near the Bazaar at Deva, I want the same share as each of you are getting, after paying off the Shifter."

It still wasn't making sense.

"So why haven't you just gone after the cow on your own, before now?"

"Honestly," she said, looking directly into my eyes while answering, "my father thought you, Skeeve, were the first one he had ever sold the map to that had a chance of actually getting to the cow."

"You didn't answer his question either," Aahz said. "And why should we give you such a large share of the treasure?"

She laughed. "Besides getting you out of this place? This is only one of the problems you face. My father tried a number of times to go the distance before he sold the map the first time, but he always had to turn back. There are many problems ahead. I know what they are. You need me."

"And your father thinks Skeeve can make it?" Tanda asked.

I would have been unhappy with the sound of disbelief in Tanda's voice if I didn't feel exactly the same way.

Glenda reached over and touched my hand on the table.

Electric shocks went up my arm and I am sure my face again turned a bright shade of red. I couldn't even begin to think about moving my hand away from hers. And I didn't want to. She was doing things to me I had only dreamed about, all with a single touch of her hand.

"My father has the ability to see the true nature of people," Glenda said, "and their true strengths."

She rubbed the top of my hand and it was everything I could do to not let out a long, loud sigh.

"If he thinks Skeeve can get to the golden cow and win over the problems that lie ahead, then I believe in Skeeve as well."

I just smiled at Aahz, giving him my widest grin. In all our time together, I had never seen him look so disgusted.

It felt wonderful.

And so did Glenda's hand on mine.

Okay, so there was tension in the small cabin. Lots of it, of all kinds. I have to admit that having a girl my age along on this crazy quest sounded just fine by me. Especially one that thought I was special without really knowing me, and could make my entire body tingle at the touch of a hand. I liked the advantage of that. With her, I didn't have any past mistakes to climb over or make up for.

Aahz and Tanda, on the other hand, weren't so certain about taking Glenda along and cutting her in on the possible prize. And that wasn't good tension at all. And since none of us knew her, there was that tension as well.

But the way I figured it, there really wasn't much choice. Tanda couldn't hop us back to any dimension she knew of. It was just too far, and we didn't dare just risk hopping dimensions trying to get close enough. We would end up lost, or more likely dead from something like those snakes or creepy identical-people on that street.

We needed Glenda. And besides, I wanted her along. It would be fun getting to know her.

"So now there's four of us," I said, smiling across the table at Glenda and ignoring the scowls coming from my mentor.

"Great," Glenda said. "You won't regret it."

I doubted I would either.

"We split the treasure four ways," Aahz said, making the deal clear.

"After the Shifter's part is taken out," I reminded him.

"Yeah, after the Shifter's twenty-five percent."

He almost spat the last few words of the sentence as he glared at Tanda.

"There'll still be more than enough for everyone," Glenda said as she offered everyone some fresh bread. "If we can get to the golden cow and make it ours."

I took a large piece and them some of the wonderful apple jelly she had on the table. After one bite I knew that fresh bread and jelly was the best-tasting thing I remembered having in a long, long time. It more than melted in my mouth as it turned my taste-buds into a wonderful world of flavors. Man, if Glenda could make all the food she cooked do that, I was never leaving her side.

After we were all eating—and I noticed that even Tanda and Aahz enjoyed the bread—Glenda looked at me. "Dig out the map and let's figure out where we're headed next."

I pointed to Aahz. "I'm letting the big guy carry it."

I thought Aahz would choke on the bread.

Tanda laughed, and the tension in the room eased a little.

Aahz took out the map and unfolded it on the table.

Glenda moved around so that she stood beside Tanda. I scooted over to get a better look as well.

Again the map had changed.

No surprise there. We were on Vortex #6, which was now clearly highlighted on the map. There were four lines from our dimension headed to four different places. I didn't like the sounds of the four dimensions at all.

Febrile was the one on the right, Hostile the next one, Durst the next, and Molder the farthest left.

Tanda shook her head. "I don't know any of them."

"Neither do I," Aahz said.

"No way that you could," Glenda said. "They are even farther removed from Deva than this place."

She glanced at me to make sure I was listening, then pointed to Febrile.

"That place's coolest temperature is over one hundred and twenty. We wouldn't last five minutes there."

"Nice that the map designer put it on the map," I said.

"Traps," she said. "The Cartograms loved to make these sorts of things."

"Cartograms?" I asked.

She gave me another of her wonderful smiles.

"They are an entire race who explore and map dimensions, and any time they find a treasure, they do one of these treasure maps to the location of the treasure, and then sell the map."

"I'd heard about them," Tanda said. "Never bothered to buy a map from one of them, though."

"They have booths in the Bazaar at Deva," Aahz said. "Never had the need to use their services."

"Did they do the map on the wall in the Shifter's tent?" I asked.

Glenda nodded. "I'd bet that any kind of map that shows different dimensions was done by a Cartogram. Every treasure map they do is magik and often contain puzzles and traps just like this one."

"Good to know," I said, glancing at Aahz. It was clear he hadn't known about the traps when we started out after this golden cow.

My mentor just frowned at me.

Glenda went on. She pointed at the dimension with the name Hostile.

"We don't even want to think about going there. Makes Febrile look cool."

Aahz nodded.

Glenda pointed to the next one. "Durst no longer exists. Something destroyed the entire dimension thousands of years ago."

"That leaves Molder," I said. "What's it like?"

"Only been there for a few moments with my father, tracking what happened to this map three buyers ago," Glenda said, shaking her head. "It's a dark, damp place where everything always seems to be changing. Even the ground seems to grow and move under your feet."

"So tell me," Tanda said to Glenda. "You've gone after this treasure with your father, and seen others do it. You must know the path at least a few steps ahead. Why can't we just jump over this step. Don't you know where the map will lead us?"

I had to admit that Tanda had a good point there. It would sure be a lot easier.

Glenda sighed, and even the sigh was a wonderful sound to my ears. She could sigh at me all she wanted.

"I wish I could," Glenda said.

"The map is magik," Aahz said. "It's never the same. Right?"

"Exactly," Glenda said. "Except for going through these Vortex locations at one point or another, the map changes the correct path with every user, and every attempt."

"Hmmm." Aahz said, staring at the piece of parchment. "Too bad we can't just take the magik out of the map and have it tell us the only true path to the dimension with the golden cow."

That gave me an idea. It was so simple it was probably stupid, so I didn't say anything aloud. Still, the thought kept rattling around in my head as the others continued their conversation.

What if I tapped into the magikal energy of the map, just like I did with the energy lines when I was casting a spell? Wouldn't that draw off the magik?

I made myself relax, then reached out with my mind and touched the map Aahz was holding, working at absorbing energy as I did.

At first nothing happened. Then the parchment began to tremble and an energy line sprang into being, running from the map to me.

It was a cool, tingly sensation, but strong, almost too strong, and getting stronger and stronger. I quickly opened up, letting the energy channel through me and into the ground, just as Aahz had taught me in some of our earliest lessons.

"What the..." Aahz exclaimed, letting go of the map.

Instead of falling, it hovered in midair.

"Skeeve!" Tanda shouted, but I ignored her, keeping my attention on what I wanted to happen.

Finally the energy flow slowed and ebbed until it was merely a trickle. I released my mental contact, and the parchment fluttered to the floor.

"Try looking at it now," I said.

All three of them were looking at me as if I had suddenly grown another head.

"Someone want to explain to me what just happened?" Glenda said, taking her gaze away from me to look back at the map.

Aahz frowned as he did the same.

Tanda laughed. "Master Magician Skeeve here just solved a whole bunch of our problems."

I stared at the map, not believing what I was seeing.

Now there was only one line from Vortex #6 to Molder, then a line from Molder to Vortex #5, then a line to a dimension called Baasss, then a line back to here, Vortex #6, then one final line to our cow dimension.

And the cow dimension now had a name.

Kowtow.

We could jump directly from here to Kowtow.

Glenda laughed and gave me the best hug I could ever remember. Her entire body pressed into mine, and I tingled in more places than I ever wanted to admit.

"My father was right," she said as she squeezed me even harder. "You really are special."

The sound of Aahz snorting didn't take away one bit of my enjoyment of the moment.

Chapter Five

"That's wild!"
J. WEST

"What kind of name is Kowtow?" I asked, pointing at our destination on the map after Glenda released me from the hug of the century.

No one answered me.

"How did you do that?" Glenda asked, staring at me. "I've never heard of anyone taking the magik out of a treasure map before."

Her beautiful brown eyes were huge and there was a look of what I took to be slight worry. Then I realized that what I was seeing wasn't worry. She was in awe of me. And having someone in awe of me was not a circumstance that often happened.

"Honestly," I said to her, "I'm not sure."

"Why is that no surprise?" Aahz said, his eyes rolling in disgust.

"Aahz said something about taking the magik out of the map," I said, going on, explaining to her what had happened while ignoring Aahz, "So I gave it a try. I tapped into its energy like I would a force line and just let it flow through me and into the ground. That's all I did. Honest."

Tanda looked as if she understood, but was saying nothing.

"The vortex dimensions are known to be powerful places for magik," Glenda said. "That's why no one lives here very long."

"So while we're here," Aahz said, glaring at me, "be careful!"

I pointed at the map. "What? Didn't I help?"

"I think you did," Tanda said. "Glenda, do you know this Kowtow dimension? Or do we have to go back to the Shifter to get there?"

Aahz moaned at the mention of the Shifter.

"I've been there a number of times," Glenda said. "Never thought of it as a place with a great treasure, though."

"Are there cattle there?" Aahz asked.

"More than you could ever imagine," Glenda said.

"So our next adventure," I said, smiling at Glenda, "is finding a single cow in a proverbial haystack of cows."

A puzzled frown came over her face, telling me clearly she had no idea what I had just said, and since I had no idea what a cow looked like, I didn't want to try to explain a haystack of them to her.

"What our young friend there was trying to say," Tanda added, "is that if there are a lot of cows, how are we going to find the one that gives golden milk?"

Glenda shrugged. "I have no idea. No one has ever gotten this far with this map before. It would have never occurred to me that the map led to Kowtow."

Aahz wasn't adding anything, so I figured it was safe to say what I was thinking.

"Wouldn't a cow that gave golden milk live in a golden palace?"

Again they just all three stared at me.

"More than likely," Tanda said, nodding slowly.

Silence again filled the small cabin. At that point I figured it was better to just eat more bread and leave the thinking up to them.

After an hour of planning and talking, at Aahz's suggestion, Glenda dimension-hopped us to Kowtow, to a location isolated enough that we wouldn't be seen by anyone. He figured that way we would have time for me to get us in disguises so that we looked like the local residents.

Before we hopped, Aahz made real sure that either Glenda or Tanda could hop back to this cabin. And he had Glenda help him set his D-Hopper so he could as well. It seemed I was the only one who didn't have an emergency getaway. I planned on making sure I was always close to one of them. Preferably Glenda.

After the hop, we ended up standing near a large rock cliff face. The air was warm and dry, and the sun was high overhead at the moment.

The area around us looked like desert, but the ground sloped away from us down to a lush, green valley. A road came over the hill beside the cliff, wound past where we were, and down the hill to what looked to be a small town built out of wood. From what I could tell there was no building over two stories tall. The buildings seemed to be centered around the main street.

"That town is called Evade," Glenda said. "Mostly cowboys and bars."

"Cowboys?" I asked. Since I had no idea what a cow looked like, I couldn't imagine what a boy cow would be, or why they would build a town.

"Cowboys are men who take care of the cows," Glenda said. "For some reason they're called that in just about every dimension there are cows or cattle."

I wanted to ask her what a woman who took care of cows was called.

"In this dimension," Glenda said, "the cowboys are a strange bunch, let me tell you."

Aahz stood, staring at the town in the valley below them. "In what way?"

Glenda shrugged. "They seem to treat the cattle almost like they were sacred. They never hurt a cow, they never push a cow too hard, and they always talk nice to the cattle. And they protect them against anything."

"Now that *is* weird," Tanda said.

"Why?" I asked.

Aahz looked at me with one of his looks that said I was asking too many questions. I knew that look well, since I saw it two or three times a day.

"Because, in most dimensions, cows are nothing but food. Here, killing a cow is a hanging offense."

"So what do these cowboys look like?" I asked.

For once, courtesy of my earlier adventures, I knew what a hanging offense was. In fact, I knew about it intimately enough to not want to dwell on the memory.

"Actually, in this dimension, they look a lot like the three of us." Glenda laughed. She glanced at Aahz. "We're going to have to do something about you, though, big boy. They don't know about demons here, let alone Pervects."

Aahz said nothing. I think he was just glad she didn't call him a Pervert, as so many did.

Suddenly, over the hill behind us, along the road, there was the sound of something coming. Glenda had us move back behind some rocks at the base of the cliff and watch. I made sure I had a pretty good view of the road so that I could disguise us all in the right clothes.

A minute later, two men appeared at the top of the rise. They were on horses and were headed slowly down the hill toward the town below. They both were dressed pretty much the same. They had on plaid shirts, jeans-like pants, high boots, and wide belts. Their skin was tan from a long time in the sun, and they wore wide-brimmed brown hats on their heads. One was a little older than the other and both had short hair and mustaches. They rode side-by-side in silence. After they got a distance down the hill, Tanda turned to me.

"Get what they look like?"

"Easy," I said.

Pulling in the energy I needed, I changed all of us into our local disguises. I gave us all black hats, and basically similar plaid shirts. Since I couldn't see beyond the clothes what my magik did when I disguised someone, I glanced at Glenda.

"How do we look?"

"Perfect," she said. "Even Aahz's tan is red instead of green."

"Are we going to need horses?" I asked. "I can't do them."

"We might," Glenda said, looking frustrated. "Especially if the golden cow isn't close by. We might have to do some traveling, and, from what I remember, horses are the only means of travel here."

"Money?" Aahz asked. "We're going to need money as well."

"I don't think so," Glenda said. "This place doesn't use money."

I thought Aahz was going to have a heart attack. It was like telling him the sun would never come up again.

"So what do they use to trade and buy things with?" Tanda asked, also shocked at the very idea.

"Work," Glenda said. "Work is their capital."

Now I was just as lost as Aahz and Tanda looked.

Glenda went on. "You work for someone when you want something from them. They keep everything on IOU's. So if you want a drink or some food, you sign an IOU and then later you have to work off the debt."

"This *is* a strange place."

Glenda agreed and we started off down the hill, four strangers walking into a town full of cowboys. I just hope my disguises worked. Just in case, I stayed real close to Glenda. Not that that was a hardship or anything.

The town of Evade was active and primitive. The only street was appropriately enough called Main Street. It was dirt and hardened mud and very rough. It split two rows of wooden buildings with covered wooden sidewalks in front of them. Outside the main street were houses scattered through the farmlands, tucked into groves of strange-looking trees.

Music and laughter were coming from a number of the doors along Main Street. Bright-colored signs were over some of the doors, with names like Battlefield, Wild Horse, and Audry's. I had no idea what any of those names meant.

Horse-drawn wagons and single horses were tied up on rails along the wooden sidewalks, and the entire town smelled like horse droppings, of which there were some pretty good-sized piles spaced along the road.

A man with a white hat and a big shovel was slowly picking up fresh horse leavings and tossing them onto the piles. I wanted to ask him what debt he was trying to pay off, or what he was trying to buy, because whatever it was, the price was too high.

When we reached the main area of town we stepped up on the sidewalk on the left side and into the shade. Suddenly I realized just how hot our walk from the cliff had been, and how lucky it was these people wore hats. The sun hadn't seemed that hot at first, after coming from Vortex #6, but now that we were in the shade, I realized how bad it was.

We strolled along the wooden sidewalk, trying to look as if we belonged. Of course, in a town that couldn't have more than a few hundred full-time residents, four newcomers stood out like a bad blister in new shoes.

"Howdy," the first man we passed said to us. He tipped his hat and just kept right on moving.

By the time I tipped my hat back, he was past us.

A woman in long skirts and a flower-patterned blouse walked past us a few moments later.

"Howdy," she said.

I tipped my hat, as did Aahz.

She smiled at us, showing some pretty strange-looking teeth.

After she was past us I glanced down at my neck to make sure the Translator Pendant that Tanda had given me was still there. It was, but it couldn't be working, because I had no idea what "howdy" meant.

I glanced at Tanda who just shrugged.

About a quarter of the way up the street into the town we stopped and leaned against a wooden wall and tried to look as if we were relaxed. No one was bothering us, or even paying us much attention. Across the street, high-energy music was coming out of the door labeled Audry's. I could see a number of people through the open door sitting at tables. It looked like a bar or restaurant of some sort.

"Now what?" Glenda asked, studying the man in the street who was picking up horse droppings.

"We're going to need information," Tanda said.

"And we just can't come out and ask for it," I said.

Everyone agreed.

"We're also going to need horses," Glenda said. "Unless you want to do more walking in this heat."

I glanced down the street at the open countryside beyond the limits of the small town. Walking back out into that for any distance would be a very bad idea.

We all agreed that we didn't want to do that as well.

"Well, we need two things," I said. "Information about the golden cow, and horses to get us to the treasure."

"Skeeve and I will try the place across the street," Glenda said. "You two head for another one farther along."

"All right," Aahz said, surprising me by agreeing to Glenda's plan. "We meet back in the cabin on Vortex #6 in one hour."

I made sure Glenda understood, since she was my ride out of here. Then we stepped into the street, making a wide turn around one of the large piles of horsepoop the guy was collecting.

He just smiled at us and said, "Howdy."

I tipped my hat at him and he seemed satisfied enough to go back to work.

I was right in all fashions about Audry's Place. It was clear as we went through the door that it was both a restaurant and a bar. The bar was wooden and long, stretching the entire length of the left wall as we entered. A hatless guy wearing a white apron stood behind the bar, a rag in his hands.

Three of the tables were occupied with a total of ten patrons, all of them eating what looked to be large plates of vegetables. The music was loud and had a pretty good beat to it. It seemed like it was coming from a piano in the back, only there was no one sitting at the piano.

Every person in the place glanced up at us as we entered, then went back to eating and talking as if they saw strangers every day and just didn't care. I considered that a good sign.

"Howdy, folks," the guy behind the bar said, wiping a spot off the wood surface in front of him. "What's your pleasure?"

I had no idea what the guy meant. I sort of understood the words, but standing in the middle of a bar, I sure didn't understand why he was asking me about pleasure. Just a little too personal a question for someone I didn't know.

I glanced at Glenda, who seemed confused for a moment as well. Then she indicated I should follow her lead as she stepped toward the guy.

Glenda nodded her head at the bartender, sort of like tipping her hat as we reached the wide bar.

"A little something to drink, a little food, and a decent way to work off the debt." Clearly it had been the right thing to say, since the guy smiled like he had just hit the jackpot.

"Strangers are always welcome in my place," he said, reaching behind him and getting two glasses off the counter on the back wall. He put them on the bar and looked at Glenda, then me. "What'll wet your whistle?"

At that moment I was really glad that Glenda was doing the talking. I was fairly certain he was asking what we wanted to drink, but I wasn't totally certain, and I had no idea what he had to offer that could do that to a whistle.

"Oh," she said, "whatever you have will be fine with us."

The guy grabbed a large bottle of orange liquid and filled both glasses to the top. Then he slid them to the edge of the bar in front of us.

"Thank you, kind sir," Glenda said.

Again the guy beamed.

"Just grab a seat and I'll rustle you up some of my best grub."

At that moment I wanted to bang my translator pendent on the bar to make it work right.

"Nothing special," she said, smiling at the guy and winking.

He beamed again, his face red as he turned and headed for a back room. It seemed Glenda could charm just about any guy, no matter what dimension. I wasn't sure how I felt about that.

She picked up her orange drink, indicated that I do the same, and then headed for a table in the corner, a little ways away from the rest of the patrons. I followed her, taking a chair with my back to the wall so I could see everything going on.

After we were both seated I whispered to her, "You can understand him?"

She shrugged. "Mostly going with the flow."

"So we're going to have to eat grubs," I whispered, "to go with the flow?"

I had never eaten a grub, and wasn't excited about having my first now.

She laughed and patted my hand. "I think 'grub' means food in this dimension."

"Well, that's a relief."

"Yeah, isn't it."

I took a tentative sip of my drink and damn near spat it all over the table. It wasn't orange juice at all. It tasted like pulped carrots. Sour-tasting carrots.

"Interesting," Glenda said after taking a drink. Then she turned to me and made a face that only I could see. She didn't much like it either.

I glanced around at the other patrons in the place. Everyone had a glass of the carrot drink in front of them. It looked as if it was the only drink the place served.

At that moment the guy came out of the back room carrying two plates. With a smile and a flourish he slid them in front of us.

Vegetables. Asparagus, carrots, celery, a few sliced tomatoes, and part of a cucumber, artfully arranged on a bed of what looked like grass.

"Wonderful," Glenda said, smiling at the man with her biggest and most alluring smile. "I hope we can find a way to repay you for this feast."

The guy had the common decency to blush.

"I'm sure we will work something out."

At that he beat a hasty retreat to the bar.

Fingers seemed to be the preferred method of getting the food from the plate to the mouth, so I picked up one piece of celery and bit into it. It was soft, not fresh, and had a faint taste of horsedung.

I hope I managed to swallow it without looking too insulting to anyone who could see me.

Glenda tried a piece of cucumber. I could tell it wasn't good either from how slowly she chewed and then forced herself to swallow.

"We're in a vegetarian dimension," I whispered as Glenda gave the bartender an okay sign that the food was good. "What do they do with all the cattle you claim are here?"

"I have no idea," Glenda whispered. "But if I have to eat or drink any more of this garbage I think I'm going to be sick."

"Yeah, me too."

"Pretend to eat and I'll see if I can get some answers," she said.

She stood and moved over to where the man stood behind the bar. I couldn't tell what she was saying, but after a moment he laughed and looked at me as if I were the brunt of a joke. I pretended to bite and chew on a asparagus spear and just smiled back.

At that moment Aahz and Tanda came in. They glanced first at Glenda, then saw me and came over and sat down in the other two chairs, their backs to the main part of the room.

"Started without us, I see," Tanda said.

"Couldn't resist," I said loud enough for the bartender guy to hear. Then I whispered, "This stuff is awful."

"What is she doing?" Aahz asked, his voice a barely audible whisper.

I pretended to eat a tiny bit of grass, covering my mouth as I answered him.

"Getting information. And for heaven's sake, don't order the food. You have any luck?"

"None," Tanda said.

A few seconds later the bartender pointed down the street in the opposite direction from where we had entered the town. Glenda smiled and came back over.

"Horses are sold down at a stable just outside the edge of town," she said. "I told him we'd clean the kitchen for our food and drink."

"I wonder what we'll have to do for horses?" Aahz asked, shaking his head.

Glenda shrugged and kept pretending to eat.

"Besides," I said. "We don't know where we're going yet."

"True," she said.

"That's our biggest problem," Aahz said.

Suddenly it dawned on me that we *should* know where we were going. What kind of magik map would simply lead to a dimension without giving directions to the location of the treasure in the dimension? After all, a world was a very large place to be looking for one cow.

I had taken the magik out of the map as far as getting to this crazy dimension. But it hadn't occurred to us to check the map once we were here.

"Aahz," I whispered. "Check the map."

He frowned at me. "Why would I—"

He must have had the same thought I had. Maybe, just maybe, the magik was back for local directions.

He reached into his pouch and pulled out the parchment. Since his back was to the bar, he kept the map in front of him so no one else in the place could see it. Then, slowly, he opened it.

It was instantly clear to me, as I pretended to love a hunk of cucumber, that the map had again changed. It was no longer a dimension map, but now a map of Kowtow.

The customers closest to us finished off their veggie plate and got up to leave. That left only two other tables and the guy behind the bar. And at the moment he wasn't looking.

"Open it all the way and see where we are," Glenda said. "It's clear."

Aahz, much to his credit, didn't turn around to check to see if she was right. He simply opened the map and spread it out over our plates of bad food.

No one paid any attention.

The golden cow palace was marked on the map. Well, at least we knew where *that* was.

Evade, the town we were in now was also marked. The road between them was marked as the lines between dimensions had been marked. There were a lot of other towns along the way, and one thing was very, very clear. We were still a long way from the golden cow.

Glenda studied the map hard, almost as if she were memorizing it.

"See anything that will help?" Tanda asked.

"If we go back to Vortex #6 I can get us a lot closer."

"Thank heavens," I said.

"Don't be thanking anyone yet," she said, staring at the map. "It's still going to be too far to walk."

Aahz folded up the map, put it back in his pouch, and stood.

"Tanda and I will go find a secluded place to hop back," he whispered, leaning forward so only the three of us could hear him. "Think you two can get out of here without being noticed?"

"Easy," Glenda said.

"See you there," Tanda said, standing and moving toward the front door.

After we had pretended to eat more of our lunch, pushing the stuff into a pile on one side of the plate like I used to do as a kid, Glenda got up and went back over to the guy behind the bar.

I kept pretending, wishing the stuff tasted good, since the idea of eating had made me hungry.

After a moment the guy in charge nodded to Glenda, smiling as if she had promised him more than I wanted to think about.

She motioned that I should join her and I did, carrying our plates. The guy led us through the door and into what might be called a kitchen. There were barrels of the different veggies against one wall, and some dirty plates and glasses stacked near a water barrel. No wonder everything tasted so bad. I didn't want to even think about the fact that I had eaten a bite of some of the stuff from this room.

"Wash water is in the barrel," he said. He tossed me a dirty towel. "Dry the dishes before wiping down everything else."

Glenda put her hand on his shoulder and eased him around toward the door.

"Don't worry," she said. "We'll get everything all cleaned up."

"I know you will," he said. The guy was more putty in her hands than I was, and for some reason that thought just annoyed me.

He went back out through the door and Glenda turned to face me.

"Well, handsome, my father was right. You are special."

I could feel myself blushing. "Thanks."

"No, thank *you,*" she said, "for everything. In all the years of trying to find the silly treasure on that map, I never thought I'd know exactly where it was at."

"Well, now we do, and we can get there pretty soon," I said. "Jump us back to Vortex #6."

She smiled and shook her head.

"Sorry, my prince in a white hat. Maybe next time."

With a slight wave and a kiss motion, she vanished in a slight POOF!

"That's not funny," I shouted, staring at where she had been.

The guy came in, looking puzzled.

"What's not funny? And where is your beautiful friend?"

I glanced around, then pointed at the back door.

"I told her I'd get started on the dishes. She'll be right back, I'm sure."

"Good," he said. "Let me know when she returns. She said she had a surprise for me."

He headed back out into the main room, leaving me standing there alone in a strange kitchen.

In a strange dimension.

It seemed he wasn't the only one Glenda had planned a surprise for.

Chapter Six

"Alone again...naturally."
R. CRUSOE

Now I have to admit that my first reaction after Glenda left me standing there in that restaurant kitchen was to scream and shout and call out her name, along with Aahz and Tanda's names.

Screaming would have covered up the panic I felt, but I knew for a fact that screaming would have done no good. But I still wanted to, more than anything.

I didn't.

My second reaction was to run like crazy out the back door, but then I would be a wanted man for skipping out on the lunch bill, and considering I might be stuck here for some time, I managed to not run either.

But I sure wanted to.

The third reaction I had was to go into automatic to give my poor mind time to sort through what had just happened. That was as good as anything I could do, so I turned and started washing off the dishes, dumping the garbage in a big pail, and dipping the plates enough in the dirty barrel water that they pretended to be clean.

I could imagine that on the outside I looked calm and collected, but on the inside I was a mess.

"Don't panic. Don't panic. Don't panic," I kept saying to myself, timing the phrase with deep breaths and the dipping of the dishes in the water.

Finally I got myself under enough control to ask a few questions.

Why had she left me?

No easy answer. At least none that I wanted to really admit, yet there was nothing else that made sense. She had left. That simple. She had seen the location of the golden cow treasure and that was the last thing she needed from me or Aahz or Tanda. On the first opportunity she had headed off on her own.

Leaving me alone in a kitchen in a strange dimension.

"Don't panic," I said to myself, dipping more dishes.

I dumped more half-eaten food into the bucket, dipped another plate, and asked the next question.

Had I been a fool?

The answer to that one came clearly in Aahz's voice.

Yes.

He would also say it was nothing new or unusual. She had played me, and Aahz and Tanda, like a finely tuned musical instrument, using my heart and my emotions as the strings.

"What a fool," I said aloud.

There was no one in there to agree with me, but I didn't need anyone to agree. I knew I had been a fool.

I scraped, dipped, and went on to the next question.

What do I do now?

I had no idea.

Nothing. I was stuck here for the moment. Maybe forever if something happened to Aahz and Tanda, or if they couldn't find me.

The thought made me panic, so I kept washing dishes.

After a few minutes the guy came back in with more dirty plates. He was clearly disappointed that Glenda was not back yet, but he said nothing. He put the plates down and then left.

I dumped the awful food and dipped the plates, doing my best to keep calm. But pretty soon I was out of dishes to wash. I used the dirty rag to wipe off all the plates and stack them, then I wiped off the counter as well. After I was done I couldn't think of anything else to do, so I went back out to the bar.

"My friend came in a few minutes ago," I said.

He looked as if he might cry, so I went quickly on with my lie.

"She said she will be back in about an hour with your surprise."

That brightened him right up again.

"You want to check what I have done back there?"

"Nope," he said, smiling. "Everything is even with you as far as I'm concerned."

"Great grub you got here," I said, patting my stomach and then tipping my hat.

"Thanks, partner," he said, smiling and showing me the same ugly-looking teeth the woman had. "Anytime. You come back now, ya hear?"

"Sure will," I said, and headed out into the street.

The sun was still cooking the hard center of the street, so I stayed on the sidewalk, tipping my hat and saying "Howdy" to anyone who passed me. The guy with the shovel must have finished cleaning up the street, leaving only the big piles of horse droppings as evidence of his work.

It hadn't been much longer than fifteen minutes since Glenda had left me, even though it felt like an eternity. There was no sign of her or Aahz or Tanda.

I kept moving, fighting down the desire to shout out Aahz's name. And the desire to just run. I didn't know where I would run, but for some reason running was a massive desire.

I reached the edge of town and stood on the last board of the covered sidewalk looking up the road that wound toward the cliff where we had hopped into this dimension. I was sure Tanda and Aahz would come back for me.

Unless, of course, Glenda had done something to them on Vortex #6.

I didn't want to think about that. If that happened, I was going to be stuck right here for a very long time.

There was no sign of anyone on the road coming down the hill. I turned and headed back up the sidewalk, doing my "Howdy" bit to anyone who passed, with the hit-tipping routine added in. When I reached the other end of town and the end of the shaded sidewalk, I stared off into the distance to where the road vanished into some low hills.

Then I turned around and started back.

At the moment there was nothing else left for me to do.

I managed to walk the entire length of the town six times before I decided that my behavior might attract attention I didn't want. When I reached the end of the sidewalk again, on the end of town where we had first entered, I sat down with my back to the wall.

Overhead the sun was slowly dropping. It didn't look like it would be more than a few hours before it set. Then what would I do?

I didn't have a clue.

The question as to why Aahz and Tanda hadn't come back for me yet bothered me a lot. I figured that with my washing dishes and pacing the length of the town, a good two hours had gone by. The pacing had helped me some, allowing me to work off some of the panic and fear. For the moment it felt as if my mind was working pretty clear again, and I was proud of myself for how well I had done so far. I just hoped I would have a chance to tell Aahz and Tanda and let *them* be proud of me.

I stared out at the empty road. The last thing I wanted was to be stuck on a vegetarian planet with some weird, hat-tipping people who didn't believe in money.

Down the street a couple people looked at me, seeming almost shocked because I was sitting on the sidewalk. I stood, tipped my hat at them, and leaned against the building instead.

They smiled as if I were now suddenly all right, and went about their business. For the next few minutes I stared out at the empty road leading off toward the rock cliffs, trying to decide what to do. Should I walk back up there or stay right where I was?

What would I do if I got to the cliff face and they weren't there, which was likely? It would be almost dark by then and I would have to spend the night out in the wild. And, for some reason, that idea didn't sit well.

And what would I do if they never came back here? Should I head for the city with the golden cow in it? I remembered enough from the map that the city's name was Dodge. I could work my way there, given time.

I'd make that decision if Aahz and Tanda didn't come back. Right now I just needed to make sure Aahz and Tanda could find me when they did get here. This little town was where they had left me; this was where I was going to stay. At least for the immediate future, however long that might be.

If Glenda *had* managed to do something awful to Aahz and Tanda, I would face that problem later. Much later. And somehow make sure Glenda paid for her sins.

With one last look at the empty road, I turned and headed back to Audry's. At least there I could sit in the window and watch the street without being obvious.

The music was still coming from what looked like a piano, even though the place was empty. The guy behind the bar smiled at me, then frowned when Glenda didn't follow me in the door.

I decided I needed to have him on my side. I walked up to the bar.

"Has my friend been back here yet?"

"No," he said. "You ain't found her?" There was instant worry in his question.

"Haven't seen her since I left here earlier," I said. "Been walking the length of your fine town looking for her."

"I was a wonderin' what you were doin'," he said. "Can't imagine what might have happened to her, though. The full moon is still a few days off, so the round-up couldn't have taken her. At least not yet."

I desperately wanted to ask him what the full moon had to do with anything, and what a round-up was, but he said both so matter-of-factly that I knew I would blow my cover if I asked.

"Yeah, couldn't be that." I said instead.

"She was askin' about horses," he said. "Maybe she got one and headed down the road?"

I shook my head. "I checked. She didn't. Mind if I just sit over there and wait?"

"Not at all," he said, reaching down and grabbing a glass. Before I could think of a reason to stop him that sounded good, he poured me another glass of the carrot juice.

"On me," he said, sliding the glass toward me across the bar. "Just tell your friend when you see her that she still owes me a surprise."

"Oh, trust me," I said. "When she promises a surprise, she *always* pays off."

He didn't know how truthful that statement was.

He beamed at that and I took my glass of juiced carrots and went over and sat down so I could see out the window. The shadows were growing long and the heat was leaving the main street of Evade. It looked as if the nights in this area were pretty chilly. I was glad I hadn't decided to go up to the cliffs just for that reason.

Let alone whatever a round-up was.

I took a sip of the carrot juice just to quench my thirst, than sat back and watched the few people still out on the street. They all seemed to have tasks and walked purposefully, tipping their hats to each other.

An hour later I had managed to sip down almost half a glass of the juice.

My bartender friend was looking a little worried, and the shadows were almost completely across the street. I figured there wasn't much more than a half-hour until sunset.

"I'm afraid I got to close up, you know," he said finally after pacing back and forth a few times near the bar. "You got a place to bunk for the night?"

I assumed bunk meant sleep, so I said, "No, haven't given it much thought."

He looked shocked. It was as if I'd told him I'd killed his mother. His mouth opened, then closed, then opened again, but no words came out.

One of the main buildings right in the center of town had a sign on it that said Hotel Evade, so I tried to cover.

"Just figuring on stopping in the hotel. Sure hope they got rooms, now that you mention it."

He looked relieved. "I'm sure they do," he said. "That's the law."

He laughed and I laughed with him, even though I had no idea what he was talking about.

"Thanks for the drink," I said, sliding the glass across the table to him and standing. "I guess it is getting dark enough for me to get going."

The promise of me leaving had him back to his old happy self.

"I'm sure your friend will get inside all right," he said. "Maybe she's already at the hotel. When you see her tomorrow, bring her by here for breakfast."

"It'll be my pleasure," I said. "And your surprise."

He laughed.

I laughed.

Then I stepped out onto the sidewalk. He slammed and latched the door behind me, bolting it as if a thousand thugs were going to try to break it down. Then the shutters on the inside of the window closed.

The shadows were long on the street and there wasn't a person in sight anywhere. Every window was shuttered, every door closed. The sound of music that had come from a few different establishments was now replaced by the silence of the coming darkness. My stomach started to clamp up, not from the little bit of carrot juice, but from worry. Something very major happened at night on this dimension. I didn't know what it might be, but it was something that made this town bolt its doors and get off the street before the sun went down. And if I was smart, I would do the same thing.

I walked to the end of town and looked up the road toward the rock cliffs. In the fading light there wasn't a soul on the road. Finding Aahz and Tanda would have to wait until tomorrow.

But I had a feeling that, with every hour, finding them was going to become less and less likely.

I turned and headed down the sidewalk toward the hotel.

The door was closed and shutters were covering the windows, but when I pounded a very nice woman behind the desk let me in. She didn't ask for anything, or even suggest something I could do to pay for my room. She just said it was lucky I got it when I did, then showed me a comfortable room on the second floor with a window that was bolted closed and the shutters drawn tight.

There was a bed, a small water basin on a dresser, and an indoor toilet down the hall.

I thanked her and she went away.

I checked to see if I could open the shutters, but they were secured solidly. Whatever was going to happen tonight, I wasn't going to be able to see it from this window.

I lay down on the fairly comfortable bed, not even bothering to take off my clothes.

Images of Tanda and Aahz floated through my mind. If Glenda had done something to them on Vortex #6 there wasn't a darn thing I could do to help. I was stuck here, without the ability to hop dimensions, in a world where everyone ate vegetables and was afraid to go out at night.

Even though there wasn't a sound from outside, it was a very long and sleepless night in that little room.

Chapter 7

"You can't go home again."
PRINCESS LEIA

At the first sign of light through the shutters, I went downstairs. The sun was barely up, the shadows still long in the street, yet the front door to the hotel was wide open and all the shutters on the windows had been retracted. These people didn't like the night, that was for sure. I desperately wanted to ask them what they were afraid of, but there just wasn't a way to ask the question without giving away the fact that I didn't belong here, in this dimension. And at the moment I had enough problems to face without bringing more down on my head. Aahz had always told me to solve one thing at a time.

The problem I had right now was that I wasn't sure I could solve any of my problems.

I went down the street to Audry's, tipping my hat to the guy with the shovel who was back in the street picking up after the horses. My old bartender friend and employer from yesterday had the door to Audry's open and the shutters retracted. I was the first customer.

"Didn't find her, huh?" he asked as I entered.

"She must have got sidetracked and stayed with a friend," I said. "She'll show up pretty soon, I bet."

He winked. "Yeah, pretty women can lose track of time."

I didn't want to think about how he came up with that.

I had decided about halfway through the night that I was so hungry, I could even eat old veggies.

"Mind if I have a small breakfast and a glass of your wonderful beverage?"

"You bet," he said, pouring me some of the carrot juice.

I looked at the glass of orange liquid. Given enough time I might actually only loathe the stuff.

"You're lucky this morning," he said. "Just got a fresh wagon-load of the best from the fields."

"Terrific," I said.

He vanished back into the kitchen and I took up my seat at the window, taking a sip of the juice. It wasn't as bad as I remembered it from yesterday, but I was sure that was because I was another day hungry. From my seat at the table I could see the entire street and all the activity along a part of it. If Aahz and Tanda came down the Main Street, I'd know it.

The bartender brought me a small plate of veggies that were actually hard and fresh. I was shocked and managed to eat them all over the next three hours, plus finish the entire glass of carrot juice. Surprisingly enough, after that I was no longer hungry.

But I was a lot more worried about ever seeing Aahz and Tanda again.

After another hour I decided that I was going to head back up to the cliffs. I offered to wash the plates and clean up the kitchen to pay for my breakfast, but my bartender friend told me to come back later, have some dinner, and do it then. I agreed, hoping I'd never see him or his kitchen again.

It took just over an hour in the mid-day heat to walk up the road to where we had first arrived in this dimension. I didn't meet anyone on the road, and the air was so hot and silent near the cliffs, it felt as if I was walking through my own tomb.

I shook myself off and tried not to let my thoughts go to the dark side of this.

I moved over to the rocks where we had hidden to watch the two guys go by. My head was sweating under my hat so that when I reached the shade near the cliff I took it off.

I was setting my hat on a rock when I saw the glint of metal tucked down in a crack in the rock. I glanced around, but no one was watching, so I leaned down and looked closer, not believing my eyes. There, tucked into an opening in one rock, was a short metal cylinder, like nothing I had seen in this dimension so far.

It was the D-Hopper.

I carefully pulled it out, noticing that a folded piece of paper came with it.

The map!

For some reason Aahz and Tanda had left me the D-Hopper and the map. More than likely they had suspected Glenda, while I had been too blind with lust or love to see anything.

I looked at the D-Hopper to make sure I wasn't hallucinating in the heat. It was real. I held it up like an idol and did a little dance of joy right there behind the rock. For the first time I had some options. I could do something instead of just waiting and hoping. The relief was almost more than I could take.

"Slow down and think," I said to myself, hearing Aahz's voice in my head as clearly as if he were standing beside me.

I took a few deep breaths of the hot air and looked out over the valley toward the town below. If Aahz and Tanda had walked up here to hide this for me, Glenda had beat them back to Vortex #6. And more than likely she had gotten the jump on them, which was what had kept them from coming back for me.

That thought took all the excitement out of the moment. I just hoped they were still alive. Glenda didn't strike me as being bloodthirsty, but I had been wrong about her before. More than likely if she considered Aahz and Tanda competition in getting the treasure, she would do something to stop them. She hadn't considered me a problem.

But something had stopped them from coming back, that much was clear. They were the ones that now needed rescuing, not me. The tables had turned and I needed to make sure I did this right. The life of my friends might depend on it.

I tucked the map in my pouch and sat on the rock with the D-Hopper on my lap, trying to make myself think what I needed to do next. The D-Hopper was set for Vortex #6. That was good, but if I went there, and couldn't find Aahz and Tanda, could I get back here? At least here I could live on carrot juice and bad veggies. I didn't give myself much of a chance on Vortex #6, even with increased magik powers in that dimension.

I had a slight working knowledge of the D-Hopper from carrying one on the shopping trip with Tanda. There was a place on the D-Hopper that set the current dimension as a return point. I carefully looked over the cylinder, then without changing the setting for Vortex #6, I set the current dimension as a return point.

I double, then triple-checked myself. If I triggered the D-Hopper I would jump to Vortex #6. If I triggered it again, I would jump back to this spot.

Okay, *that* problem was solved.

I stood and was about to hop when I remembered what I might be going into.

"Stop and think," I said aloud, again with Aahz's voice echoing through my head.

With luck, the D-Hopper would put me back into the cabin, but in case it didn't, I needed to be ready.

What happened if Glenda was still there with them? I needed something to fight her with. I picked up a good-sized rock that fit nicely in my hand. It wasn't much, but it might be enough if it came to a fight.

"Okay," I said aloud. "Anything else?"

I couldn't think of anything. And in the heavy coat I was starting to sweat more than I had before.

"Think, then act," I said, repeating what Aahz had said a hundred times. "It's time to act."

With one last look at the town of Evade down in the valley, I took a deep breath and triggered the D-Hopper.

The storm slammed into me like a hammer. I tucked the D-Hopper into my shirt and focused on how Tanda had led us the other three times to the cabin. The dust didn't let me see anything around me, but I knew there were some scattered trees. We had passed them the last two times.

Tanda had gone slightly downhill and to the right, so I figured out what I thought was directly downhill, then angled a little to the right, counting my steps to make sure that if I was on the wrong path, I could get back. After twenty steps I could see the faint shape of a tree. I was sure that had been there the last time, so I kept going.

Another thirty slogging steps and another tree loomed out of the blowing dust. I thought that had been there as well. So far so good.

I kept moving for fifty more steps before I saw the faint light in the window of the cabin below me. I had almost missed it, walking too high along the hillside.

I eased my way down to the cabin and tried to look in the window, but the dirt and shades made it so that I couldn't see anything.

It looked as if I was going to have to go in, hard and fast, like a soldier going after a dangerous outlaw.

I got to the door, braced myself, and eased open the door latch then shoved hard, the rock from Kowtow ready in my hand as I stumbled in.

My momentum pushed me three steps into the room before I caught my balance and stopped. I had the rock raised to hit at Glenda, who I expected to be standing there, ready to fight me.

She wasn't there.

The cabin was warm and comfortable, just like the last time I had seen it.

Tananda and Aahz were sitting at the table, eating what smelled like beef stew with slices of homemade bread.

"Nice entrance," Tanda said, smiling at me. "What took you so long?"

Aahz just shook his head.

"Shut the door, would you?"

I stood there with the rock in the air over my head, not really believing what I was seeing. I had so convinced myself that Aahz and Tanda were in trouble that I couldn't believe that they were simply having lunch and waiting for me. Why had they let me stay the entire day and night in Kowtow?

Why had they chanced that I would even find the D-Hopper where they had left it?

"Door!" Aahz said. "You born in a barn or something?"

Behind me the storm was raging, blowing dust into the cabin. I lowered the rock, tossed it out into the dust, and then closed the door.

Tanda stood and came up to me, smiling.

"Aahz, I told you he'd make it just fine," she said, giving me a hug that convinced me that she was just fine, and I wasn't dreaming all this.

Aahz snorted. "After all the mooning over our friend Glenda, I didn't think his brain would ever work again."

I asked the one question I wanted to know most of all.

"Why didn't you come back?"

"We couldn't," Tanda said, patting me on the back and leading me to the table, where she slid some bread toward me as I sat down.

I stared at my mentor, who was just eating and not paying much attention to me at the moment. He did that when he was very angry or very happy, and at the moment I honestly didn't know which it was.

"Stew?" she asked, holding up a pot of what was making the room smell so good. "Glenda left us enough food to last for a few weeks at least."

"Nice of her," Aahz said, the anger clearly there.

"When you didn't come back for me I thought you were both dead."

"We would have been dead in four or five weeks," Aahz said. "When the food ran out."

Tanda served me up a dish of the stew and then sat down next to me after patting my shoulder.

"So why couldn't you come back?" I asked, not wanting to eat until I had some answers. "What happened?"

"Well," Aahz said, still not looking at me, "we both knew Glenda was up to something, and was going to try to double-cross us."

"And we expected her to leave you on Kowtow," Tanda said.

"You expected that?" I was stunned and suddenly angry. "Why didn't you at least warn me?"

Aahz looked me directly in the eye. "Would you have listened, apprentice?"

"Yes," I said defensively.

Now they both laughed.

Clearly they thought I had been too much under Glenda's spell. And the more I thought about it, the more I saw that they were right, at least to a point. When Glenda started her act on the bartender, I started to get suspicious, but not enough to think it through.

"You were the closest to her, apprentice," Aahz said, his voice stern and in lecture mode. "You should have been warning us about her, not the other way around."

As normal, Aahz was right.

"So what happened here?" I asked, trying to not admit I had been wrong, even though we all knew I had been.

"We headed up to the rocks and left the D-Hopper and the map," Tanda said, "then I jumped us here."

"And right into Glenda's waiting arms," Aahz said. "Just as she had been planning."

"She used a dimension-blocking spell on me," Tanda said. "She searched us for the D-Hopper, wished us both luck when she couldn't find it or the map, and hopped out."

"I assume she's going after the treasure," Aahz said. "And now she's got a full day's start on us." So what I had been feeling from Aahz was anger, both at me and at the fact that we might lose the treasure, after getting so close.

"So what's a dimension block?"

"A spell that keeps another person from jumping out of a dimension," Aahz said. "Some cultures use it to imprison people. It's a pretty basic spell."

"That you haven't taught me yet," I said.

He shrugged. "There's a lot I haven't taught you. And after falling so easily for this Glenda's charms and smooth talk, I'm not sure if I ever will."

Tanda patted Aahz's green hand across the table.

"Easy on your apprentice. He's young and full of hormones. He *did* get back here, didn't he?"

I wanted to ask what a hormone was, but figured I'd get that information from Tanda later, when Aahz wasn't around to make fun of my stupidity. He was disgusted enough with me as it was. And this time around I agreed with him. I shouldn't have been so easily taken with Glenda. She'd given me a couple of compliments and I'd been putty in her hands.

I looked at Tanda. "So once you jump out of here with the D-Hopper, the spell is broken?"

"Exactly," she said.

"Finish up," Aahz said. "We've given her enough of a head start as it is."

"So how do we get the treasure home once we find it?" I asked, then instantly realized just how stupid my question was. It had been Glenda who had told us we were too far from any of our known worlds to dimension-hop safely. That had been another of Glenda's lies.

Tanda shook her head. "I think that's where Glenda got me. She blocked my sense of dimensions when we got near her. When we jumped back here from Kowtow, into the storm, I could sense Vortex #4 and Vortex #2. We can get home any time we want."

My relief at that, combined with my relief at finding Aahz and Tanda all right, was more than I could handle. I stared at my stew, trying to make myself eat as much of it as I could. Doing anything else and I just might fall apart completely.

"So what did you do when she left you?" Tanda asked.

I shrugged, making myself focus on what I had managed to do right.

"Paid our bill by doing the dishes so no one would be chasing me, then explored the town to see what I could see, then sat and waited, staying in the open so that you could find me."

"And slept?" Aahz said, his voice sounding disgusted.

"Not really," I said. "I got a hotel room because those people are deathly afraid of being outside at night. And of something called a round-up."

"Really?" Tanda asked.

I glanced up from my stew. Even Aahz was now showing interest.

"Yeah, they bolt their doors and shutter every window, every night," I said. "I couldn't think of a way to ask them what they were afraid of without tipping my hand that I was a demon. And at that point I had other problems to figure out, like what to do next if you two didn't come back."

Aahz nodded. "So we need to be careful at night."

"The bartender guy said the round-up was still a few days off, since it wasn't the full moon yet."

"I wonder what they're rounding up?" Tanda asked.

"Or who's doing the rounding?" Aahz added. "There's a lot to Kowtow we don't know. You have the map?"

"I sure do," I said, taking it out of my pocket and handing it to him.

As I did I had another realization. The map was magik. It hadn't shown us the right path to Kowtow until I took the magik out of it, but back on Kowtow the magik had returned to the map.

"Aahz," I said, smiling at my mentor, "you know, don't you, that the magik returned to the map when we reached Kowtow?"

"Yeah," he said, almost sneering at me. "So? Glenda saw it as well."

"Exactly," I said, smiling at my green mentor, "Glenda looked at the map while we were in Evade. Right?"

Suddenly Tanda burst out laughing, long and hard and so loud I thought she might hurt herself.

I smiled at the puzzled expression on my mentor's face. Considering how stupid I had been lately, getting back on top and giving him some good news felt good.

"The map is a puzzle," I said. "That basic nature of the map won't change just because we reached Kowtow."

Suddenly the light in Aahz's eyes brightened and slowly a smile crept over his green-scaled face.

"Glenda has the wrong location."

"Exactly," I said. "The map changes every time we get closer, just as it did with dimensions. I'm betting it will do that on Kowtow as well."

Aahz put the folded map back in his belt pouch and stood, suddenly in a hurry.

"Great thinking, Skeeve," he said. "Let's get back to Kow-tow. Glenda is going to come looking for us to get the map when she discovers she has wrong information. And when she does, I want to be ready for her this time."

I liked that idea a lot.

Chapter Eight

"Flying. It's the only way to travel!"
B. HOLLY

We arrived back at the cliff face on Kowtow with less than two hours of daylight left. The day was still hot and dry, and nothing had changed in the general area since I had left a few hours before. I quickly disguised all three of us again in the standard wear of the people of this dimension.

We had packed some food and containers of water. Aahz didn't much like the idea of eating vegetables. Pervects were mostly meat-eaters. Aahz checked over the D-Hopper and then reset the dimension and hid it in his shirt.

"Ahh, that feels good," Tanda said, stretching toward the sun, her white hat tipped back, her large belt buckle glistening in the sun.

"The heat?" I asked.

"Nope. The dimension block being lifted. Amazing how much you miss the ability to hop after you've had it and then it's taken away."

"Yeah, I know," Aahz said.

"Oh, sorry, big guy," she said.

"Gotten used to it," he said.

I couldn't even imagine how Aahz felt, once being a powerful magician and then having his powers taken away from him because of a practical joke by my previous mentor. My mentor had been killed before he could lift the joke. Now Aahz just had to wait for the joke to wear off and his powers to come back, which he said would take more time than I wanted to think about.

Aahz unfolded the magik map and laid it on the top of a rock so we could all study it.

The town of Evade was clearly marked as our starting point, with a road leading from it to a town called Baker. In Baker two roads split off to two other towns, then two roads left each of those towns. Eventually a few of the roads led to Dodge, where it was marked that the treasure was.

Where Glenda was heading.

But was the golden-milk-giving cow there? I was betting it wasn't. I was betting the map would change when we reached Baker. And then keep on changing with every city after that until we finally found the right city.

Glenda was going to be angry, and it served her right. I didn't want to see what Aahz would do to her the next time he saw her. Pervects are not to be messed with, and she had left him to die on a frozen planet. What he would do to her wasn't going to be pretty.

"So we're back needing horses," Aahz said, tracing along the distances between the towns. Then he looked at me. "Unless you think your flying spell is good enough here to work for us."

Flying wasn't the strongest of my magik, but it was one of the things Aahz had trained me to do first. It had saved us from a hanging and a few other tight spots in our last few adventures. But I wasn't sure if I could lift all three of us and carry us any distance.

"I can try," I said, wishing I hadn't said those words the moment I heard them come out of my mouth.

"Concentrate," Aahz said, going into teacher mode. "Search for your lines of power and use them, pull them in, let them flow through you."

"You can do it, Skeeve," Tanda said.

I wasn't so sure. Each place had power lines, invisible things that all magicians got their energy from. Some places, like the area of the cabin in Vortex #6 were jam-packed with power. Back at the cabin I could have flown fifty people, but here there wasn't much magik power. In fact, it seemed almost empty.

I stretched out my mind, holding onto the power that I could feel, and then concentrating on bringing it in and using it to lift all three of us. A moment later we all were off the ground and into the hot air.

"Not too high," Aahz warned. "Keep us just three or four paces off the ground."

I was glad to do that, because it was easier. And much safer to boot. I lowered all three of us back to a position just above the top of the boulders and held us there for a few moments to make sure I could do it, then I lowered us back to where we had started.

When I let us go I could feel the energy drain away. I was sweating and short of breath and needed a drink of water, but at least I had done it.

"Nice job," Tanda said, handing me a canister of water.

"How long do you think you could keep that up?" Aahz asked, watching me with a look that I knew meant he could see through any extra bragging I might try.

"Honestly, I don't know," I said after I took a long drink of the wonderfully cold liquid. "With rests, and touching each of you as I do it, maybe fifteen minutes at a time. The lines of power are weak in this area. They may be stronger in other areas and then I could last longer."

Aahz nodded, seemingly satisfied with my answer. He turned to Tanda.

"Can you do a cushion spell, in case he drops us?"

"Not a problem," Tanda said.

"What do we do if someone sees us?" I asked. "I'm not sure that I can do a bird disguise spell as well as keeping us flying."

"We're not going to worry about that," Aahz said. Clearly he didn't think I could either.

"We'll walk when we see someone," Tanda said, staring at the town below us in the valley. "Just keep us close to the ground and over a road."

I nodded. "Whenever you're ready."

"Good," Aahz said. "Take us down to Evade, we'll walk through town and out the other side."

I nodded, glancing at how low the sun was getting in the sky. We'd have to deal with where we were going to stay later.

I doubted that Aahz would want to stay in Evade. With luck we'd reach Baker, and they'd have a hotel there as well.

I moved over and stood between Aahz and Tanda, putting a hand on each of their arms. Then I concentrated on taking in what power I could find and lifting us about a pace off the ground.

"Hold on to your hats," I said as we lifted into the air.

I floated us down to the road and then picked up speed, skimming us toward Evade a lot faster than even a running horse could take us. To an outsider we must have looked very strange. Three strangers seeming to be just standing, but moving along the road at a very fast clip.

After only two minutes I was starting to feel the wear, but before I had to stop Aahz said, "I think we're close enough now."

What had cost me an hour of walking earlier had only taken two or three minutes of flying. Why hadn't I thought of that this morning?

I slowed and put us down at a normal walking pace. The moment I let go of the power I stumbled, but Tanda kept me from falling on my face. It was as if every bit of energy had been drained from my muscles, leaving them weak and noodle-like. "You'll be fine in a moment," Aahz said, keeping us walking at a good pace toward the now close edge of town.

He was right. A few more steps and I was sweating like a dam had broken, but I was able to walk.

Tanda gave me some more water, and that brought even more of my energy back. I was starting to believe that I could do this. And flying, even though it tired me out, was a lot better than riding horses, let alone doing the job it would take to pay for one.

We got into town as people were starting to close up their businesses and shutter the windows.

"You weren't kidding, were you?" Tanda said as we walked down the now mostly deserted sidewalk.

"They're afraid of something that comes out at night," I said. "I have no idea what it might be."

As we passed in front of Audry's, my friend the bartender waved from inside the window. I tipped my hat back at him. These people might be strange vegetarians who were afraid of the dark, but they sure were nice. We passed the hotel without Aahz even hesitating. And I didn't say anything either. The last thing I wanted to let my mentor know was that the fear the locals felt had gotten to me as well during my one-night stay here. On the other side of town we stepped off the sidewalk and just kept walking, past a few homes with the shutters already drawn and bolted. Ten minutes later, with the sun still not touching the tops of the hills to the west, Aahz gave the all-clear.

Again I touched each of them, pulled in the power, and lifted us, sending us down the road as fast as I dared take us, considering I had to make sharp corners and steep hills.

This time I lasted ten minutes before I had to stop. Water and a quick rest got me going again, just as the sun started to set. From what I could tell, we were a long way yet from Baker. It was getting noticeably cooler, which was also helping me.

"Can you keep going?" Tanda asked as I stopped for a second time and sat down on a rock beside the road.

"We're making good speed," Aahz said, clearly satisfied with our progress.

"We are," Tanda said, "but this is hard on Skeeve."

"I can keep going," I said, taking one more drink and then standing. "I just need to rest every ten minutes or so."

"Understandable," Aahz said. "For someone of your level of skill."

"For someone of *any* level," Tanda said, stepping to my defense. "There's not much power in this area. He's having to pull from a ways off."

"That true?" Aahz asked me.

"It is," I said. "But I said I can keep going and I can."

"Then we go when you're ready," Aahz said. "We don't have much light left and we won't be able to make the speed we are making now at night."

It was clear we were going to spend a night outside on Kowtow and face what an entire population was afraid to face.

Aahz didn't seem to be worried.

Tanda had said nothing.

I was just the apprentice. What place was it for me to say anything?

In the west the sun was slowly setting. In the east an almost full moon was starting to come up over the horizon. In a few days the full moon would signal another fear in the people who lived here: the round-up.

I pushed the thoughts and fears from my mind, focused on bringing in as much power as I could, then lifted us knee-high off the ground and headed down the road as fast as I could take us.

The sun had almost set completely by the time I stopped for my next break. There was still no sign of the town of Baker.

Okay, I'm the first to admit when I'm being stupid, if it's pointed out to me. Luckily I had had enough common sense to not tell Aahz and Tanda how worried I was about the darkness, so they didn't get the chance to point any of my stupidity when we ran into no problems at all after it turned dark.

The first part of the trip was fairly easy. It took me three more rest stops, and, it was well after the sun had set by the time we got to Baker. The town was buttoned up tighter than anything I had ever seen. In the moonlight the buildings looked haunted and strange, more like monster-boxes than structures. Very little light got past any of the shutters, but the almost-full moon was giving us enough light to see by to stay on the road.

Baker looked to be about twice the size of Evade, and was spread out over more than just a Main Street. It was tucked into a small valley, with flat farmland going off in both directions from it.

We walked into town, following the road and staying off the wooden sidewalks so that we wouldn't make any noise. The town was just flat empty. Not even a horse had been left outside. Nothing was moving, and as far as we could tell, nothing lived here, even though we knew better.

"This is *very* strange," Tanda said as we got near the center of town. "How boring would it be to go to bed when

the sun set every night? I'd go stark-raving crazy in a matter of days."

Tanda was the kind of person that always had to be doing
something: going on adventures, shopping, or partying. I had
no doubt that it wouldn't take her days to go crazy here.

"I just wonder what they are afraid of," Aahz said. He
pointed to one building. "Those shutters look as if they could
take a pretty good pounding and still hold."

"It was the same way in Evade," I said. "But I was awake
all night and never heard a sound from outside."

"More than likely this is just an old custom," Tanda said,
"and we're still so far out in the sticks, away from any larger
cities, that the custom remains."

"Are there larger cities in this dimension?" I asked.

"Who knows?" Aahz said. "Just stay alert and watch for
anything unusual."

He didn't have to tell me to do that, since I was already on
full alert. And even though flying, combined with no sleep the
night before, had me exhausted, I doubted I could sleep now
even if I wanted to try.

Aahz found a sliver of light coming from the shutters of
one store and stopped. He unfolded the map and we gathered
around, trying to be as quiet as we could while we looked for
our next destination.

"You were right, Skeeve," Aahz whispered, patting me on
the back.

The map had changed.

Baker, the city we were standing in, was now the focal
point of the map, and two roads led toward two other towns
from Baker. The treasure was now marked in a town called
Silver City. Dodge City wasn't even on the map. Glenda was
going to be mad. I wished I could be there when she discovered how stupid she had been.

"So which way do we go?" Tanda asked.

The two towns next in line from Baker were named Bank
and Keep. Both looked to be about the same distance from
here, but Bank was to the right in the north and Keep was to
the left in the south.

"Bank," I said, before I even realized the word was out of my mouth.

"Why?" Aahz asked, staring at me, his intense eyes scary in the semi-dark.

"I don't know," I said. "It just seems right, and starts with the same letter as Baker."

Tanda laughed, but had the decency to not say anything.

Aahz just shook his head, folded up the map and put it away.

"Bank it is," he said, moving out into the middle of the street and walking on toward the west end of town.

"I could be wrong," I said, walking between him and Tanda.

"More than likely," Aahz said.

"So why go with my suggestion?"

"Because I have none better to offer."

"Neither do I," Tanda said. "Besides, if you're wrong, we can blame you."

"Terrific!" I said. "As if I don't get in enough trouble as it is."

Both Aahz and Tanda chuckled, but said nothing the rest of the way to the edge of town.

It was easy to find the road to Bank. At a fork in the road a hundred paces outside of the main part of town there was a sign, clear and readable even in the moonlight, pointing to the right.

Aahz glanced around, then turned to me. "Ready?"

"Sure," I said.

"Keep it slower than before," Aahz said. "We don't want to run into anything out here."

I concentrated on the power coming into my body, easier here than back near Evade. When I had enough I lifted us slightly off the ground and headed down the road. Outside of town the road was straight, running between what looked like pastures, and even in the moonlight I could get us up to a pretty decent speed.

In the pastures along both sides of the road animals were grazing. When I finally had to stop to rest, a number of the grazing animals looked up at us, big eyes glowing in the moonlight. They almost looked surprised to see us.

"Cows," Tanda said, pointing at the large creatures staring at us from the field.

They looked fat and heavy, with white and dark areas over their bodies. In the half-darkness, they seemed almost sinister with their big eyes and long ears.

"So how come they aren't inside like everything else?" I asked as Tanda gave me more water and a little bit of a snack to eat.

"You're asking me?" she said. "Maybe they're not bothered by whatever worries the people around here."

That made sense, in an odd sort of way.

"Maybe they are what worries the residents," I said, staring into the deep pits of eyes of the closest cow.

Both Aahz and Tanda laughed as if that was the funniest thing I had ever said.

I didn't see what was so funny. Cows looked nasty to me, and I couldn't imagine trying to get milk, golden or not, from any of the ones I could see.

By the time I was rested enough to get us farther down the road, a bunch of the nearby cows had sauntered over and were gathering near the road watching what we were doing. It was creepy, and I was glad to get on the way.

From that point onward there were cattle along the road watching us, as if something had told them we were coming. When I asked Aahz what made them do that, he said he didn't know. He'd never seen cattle act that way.

Tanda said she hadn't either.

That answer didn't comfort me at all.

I kept us going longer and longer, not wanting to rest and have all the cows gather close to us. By the time the sun came up I had flown us to the edge of Bank City. I was exhausted and was going to have to get a few hours sleep before we went on.

At first light, the moment the sun peeked over the edge of the nearby mountains, the cows stopped watching us and went back to grazing.

For some reason that bothered me a lot more than them staring at us.

Chapter Nine

"It's an acquired taste."
H. LECHTER

I was so tired that even the short walk into the center of the town of Bank darned near killed me. All I wanted to do was fall down and sleep, at least for a few hours. Aahz promised me that was going to be possible very soon, so I limped along with them.

The merchants were opening up the stores and the shutters had all disappeared from the windows. Horses pulling wagons were lined up outside a few stores, and, just like in Evade, a guy wearing a hat and carrying a shovel was going around cleaning up after the horses. Clearly that was a standard job in every town. I couldn't imagine a kid wanting to be the horse-poop cleaner when he grew up. But maybe in this culture, that was the top job.

Bank looked a lot like Evade, just bigger. The buildings were all the same size, and there were wooden sidewalks.

We found a small establishment like the one Glenda had left me in, and sat down at a table near the front window. We were the only ones in the place. It felt great to be off my feet and not moving. I might be able to sleep right there in the chair if they let me.

As I looked around I realized this place was almost identical to Audry's in Evade, with the bar down the left side and wooden tables and chairs.

"What can I get for ya, folks?" A man asked as he came out from the back room.

He was just like the guy in Evade, right down to the white apron and the dirty towel.

"Could we trouble you for just one glass of your best juice?" I asked.

"Not a problem at all," he said, smiling. "You want some breakfast, I just got a fresh load in this very morning. Good and crisp."

"Sounds great," I said, "maybe later. But I think first we just want to sit a spell."

The guy came back with the carrot juice drink and slid it onto the table with a smile before he headed back into the kitchen area.

"You've picked up the lingo pretty well," Tanda said. "A night alone in a place do that for you?"

"I suppose," I said, taking a sip of the juice. "Isn't it creepy how all these people seem the same from town to town?"

"I was noticing that as well," Tanda said. "The guy shoveling dung looks just like every other guy I've seen shoveling dung."

Aahz laughed and I just stared at her, too tired to even try to figure out what she had just said.

"I wonder why there's no milk," Aahz said, staring at the carrot juice with a look of disgust on his face.

"I don't think you want to ask, even if they had any," I said. "I was in a kitchen of one of these places, and there was nothing there but veggies, and not a clean surface in the room."

"Ughh," Tanda said. "More than likely you could get us arrested for even thinking of drinking milk in a dimension full of cows."

"You two have far too active an imagination," Aahz said as he pulled out the map and opened it.

Again it had changed.

I kept sipping my carrot juice as I studied the parchment. Bank, the town we were in, was the main town on the map now. And the treasure was now located in a city called Placer. Three roads left Bank and headed off in three directions, all, in one fashion or another, getting to Placer after a few more towns.

"Now which way?" I asked, staring at our options.

They were towns called Chip, Pie, and Biscuit. Weird names. Everything about this dimension was starting to seem weird to me.

Tanda pointed to one of the towns. "Following Skeeve's plan of going to towns that start with the letter B, we head for Biscuit."

"Sounds good to me," I said.

Aahz just shook his head in amazement.

"As good as any, I suppose."

He studied the map for a moment more and then folded it up and put it away.

Biscuit was on the road that stayed north going out the west side of Bank. I doubted it would be hard to find. I took another sip while Tanda wrinkled her nose at my drink and me.

"It's an acquired taste," I said, realizing what I was doing. I had finished almost half the glass.

I offered the rest to her, but she shook her head.

"No, thanks. Not in a million years."

I shrugged and took another drink. The stuff wasn't bad at all, once you got past the initial taste of smashed and juiced carrots.

"So how you feeling?" Aahz asked.

"He's going to have to rest," Tanda said, not letting me answer.

"I know that," Aahz said. "I was just wondering how we were going to do that. We don't dare go back to the cabin because Glenda might be there. I don't want to deal with her just yet. So we have to find some private spot."

"Actually," I said, stopping the fight before it got started, "I'm feeling pretty good. A little juice here and some time sitting down and I think I can go again for a while."

Tanda looked into the orange liquid.

"What did they put in there?"

"You know," I said, looking at the juice, "I don't know, but it really is helping."

We sat for another ten minutes while I finished off the carrot juice, then I went over and asked how I could pay the man for the drink.

"Come back for a dinner," he said. "That's payment enough."

I thanked him for his hospitality. I had no idea how this bartering system in this dimension worked, but it sure made everyone friendly.

We headed toward the west end of town, walking down the sidewalk and tipping our hats at the smiling people we met. I felt great again. Drinking that juice was like getting a good night's sleep. I had no idea what was in one besides carrots, but I could easily get hooked on them.

It wasn't going to be a problem taking the wrong road because there was a sign saying Biscuit and a big arrow at the fork in the roads. Around us were buildings and homes and several hundred of head of cattle grazing, so we started off walking, going slow and steady as the sun got hotter.

Finally, after maybe a mile, we were far enough out in the country to not chance being seen flying.

"You sure you're all right?" Aahz asked.

"Never felt better," I said.

"You know, at the next town, I'm trying some of that juice," Tanda said.

As I reached out with my mind searching for power, it became clear that we were in an area much more powerful than where we had started. It was easy for me to get enough to lift the three of us knee-high off the ground and whisk us along.

We had to stop flying and walk a half dozen times over the next few hours when we saw people coming, or a house was too close to the road. And we must have passed at least a million cows along the way. Not one had actually looked at us. And not once did I have to actually sit down and rest.

Amazing juice.

By the time we reached Biscuit, it was mid-afternoon and I was starting to get tired again. We found a place to sit in a bar that looked just like Audry's and the one in Bank. Now all of us were growing bothered by the similar nature of the places. I wanted to run from the bar when a man who looked a lot like the previous two, down to wearing a white apron and carrying a dirty rag, came out of the kitchen and asked us what we wanted.

"Just two glasses of your finest," I said.

"Sure you all don't want an early dinner?" he asked. "I just got a fresh load from the fields. Really crisp. We all need our energy, you know, with the round-up coming."

I glanced at Aahz, then Tanda, then answered the guy's question.

"After we sit awhile we just might."

He smiled real big, like I had said the right thing, then went and brought us our juice. He had disappeared into the back room before any of us said anything.

"So someone want to explain to me what's going on?" Tanda asked.

"I've never seen anything like this," Aahz said. "I thought you two were just imagining things at the last stop. But these three places are almost identical."

"Are we going in circles or something?" I asked. "Is it possible that all these towns are the same one?"

"No, there're different sizes and shapes and in different countryside," Tanda said.

"No doubt we're in different towns," Aahz said, "all built, it seems, off the same pattern, with the same kind of people living in them."

"Okay," Tanda said, "now I can safely say I've seen it all."

"Not yet," I said. "We've still got the round-up, whatever that is. And a golden cow."

Tanda nodded and looked at Aahz with a serious face.

"I'm starting to think this treasure isn't worth what we're risking."

Aahz looked at her as if she had gone crazy.

"Are you kidding? We've come this far. Only a few more towns to go."

She nodded, but I could tell as I sipped my juice that this entire dimension was bothering Tanda a great deal. And in the time I had known Tanda, I had never seen anything bother her.

Aahz glanced to make sure the guy was still in the kitchen, then opened up the map and spread it on the table. As every other time, it had changed again.

This time, we had four roads to pick from, and all the towns started with the letter "B". Brae was the southern most, then there was Brawn, then Bent, and finally, to the north, Bethel. The golden treasure was marked as being in a place called Donner.

"Well, so much for that system," I said.

"And it was working, too," Aahz said.

"You know, maybe I could drain off the magik from the map again." I had just finished my entire glass of carrot juice and was feeling really, really alive and well.

Aahz glanced at the kitchen door again, then asked me, "You feel up to it?"

"I feel like I'm getting stronger the farther we come," I said.

"Let him try," Tanda said. "Might save us a lot of back-tracking."

Aahz looked at me, then nodded. "Give it a shot."

I took a deep breath and let my mind search out the power in the map. For an instant I didn't think anything was going to happen. Then I felt it. The power rushed through me from the map as I hastily directed it into the ground. My head spun for a second, and it was done. The power was gone and the map was normal...for now. I took a deep breath, again feeling the strain. I needed more carrot juice.

"It worked," Aahz said. "Nice job, Skeeve."

It wasn't often that I got a compliment from my mentor, so I savored the moment. Tanda patted me on the arm and gave me a kiss on the cheek for a reward. Nothing like doing a job and doing it well.

I took her glass of carrot juice and sipped from it while we studied the map.

Only one road led from Biscuit where we were, through Bethel and then to Donner. Donner actually was the place with the golden cow. We had been closer than we thought.

But from the look of the map, it was a long way to Bethel, and even farther to Donner. Just getting to the first place was going to take to the middle of the night. I just hoped the cows didn't watch us.

"You rested enough to get going?" Aahz asked me.

I downed half of the glass of carrot juice and nodded.

"Put this in one of our water containers, would you?"

Tanda nodded as I stood and moved to the door into the back room. I knocked and the guy came out.

"What can we do for you in exchange for the wonderful drinks you served?"

He smiled, as if I had again said some magik words.

"Just come back for food sometime soon."

"I promise we will," I said. I tipped my hat at him. "Thanks."

He stood there smiling, watching us leave like we were his children headed off to school.

We went through Bethel in the middle of the night. The town looked like all the others, and, even though it was locked up tight and shuttered, I recognized the Audry's-place-look-alike as we passed it.

For the past few hours, since a stop we made right after dark, the cows had again watched us. We were the cow entertainment for the night as we sped past pasture after pasture. Thousands and thousands of cows lined the road, ready for us to come flashing past. I had no idea why they did it, or how they knew we were coming, but there wasn't a stretch of road that didn't have cows lined up beside it all night long. And even though there were no fences, none of them came into the road to stop us.

After a while I stopped looking at them as well. Their big eyes, shining in the moonlight, just unnerved me.

My flying was getting better and better as the trip went on, and since the moon was almost full the road was easy to see. I could manage almost an hour of nonstop flying before I had to rest, and, because of the mostly flat land, we were making great time.

Even though I wanted to drink it earlier because I was feeling tired, I forced myself to wait until we were

walking through Bethel to finish the last of the carrot juice I had had Tanda save.

Just that half a glass gave me enough energy to keep on going, as if I had slept a full night. It seemed to allow me to use every bit of the power around me to keep us above the road and speeding toward the treasure.

At sunrise the cows stopped watching again, going back to grazing as if we didn't matter at all. For a while I felt almost insulted, before I realized what I was thinking. How could a cow not wanting to watch me fly past ever insult me? Made no sense.

About halfway through the morning, still a long distance from Donner, we came on a small town. It couldn't have been half the size of Evade, and not more than a dot on the map. The juice I had drunk in the middle of the night had long ago worn off and I was so tired that I was just about falling down.

As I had hoped when I saw the little town, right in the middle was a place that looked a lot like Audry's. It was empty and we went in, taking what I was starting to think of as our normal table. I slouched in a chair in front of the window, glad to still be alive.

There was only one thing bad about the carrot juice. When you came down off of it, you came down hard. Right now, if we were going to get to Donner by the middle of the night, I needed another fix or two of the golden liquor.

This place didn't just *look* like Audry's; it could have *been* Audry's. And when the guy with the white apron and dirty rag came out of the back room, I wasn't surprised in the slightest.

"What can I get for you, strangers?"

"If you wouldn't mind," I said before either Tanda or Aahz could speak, "could I trouble you for three glasses of your best?"

The guy beamed, wiped his hands with the towel, and said the words I was expecting.

"Not a problem. Sure I couldn't interest you folks in some lunch as well? Just got a fresh wagon-load in. Everything's really crisp. You all need your strength, what with the round-up coming."

"Thanks, partner," I said. "That sounds really good, but I think we'll just start with the juice right now, if you don't mind."

"Not at all," he said.

A few moments later he came back with three glasses of the carrot juice, smiled at us as he put them down, then headed off into the kitchen.

"Okay, that does it," Tanda said, staring at where the guy had gone. "I'm officially completely creeped out."

"What?" Aahz asked. "All the staring cows last night didn't do it for you?"

"Okay, *double* creeped out," Tanda said.

I downed about a half a glass of carrot juice and sat back, letting the wonderful flavor warm me. How I had ever lived without the stuff was beyond me.

"I think you might want to go easy on that juice," Aahz said. He was looking as tired as I had felt a few minutes ago.

"I think you might want to try some," I said, "if you're expecting to get to the treasure tonight."

He shook his head.

"I think one of us hooked on carrot juice is enough."

"Your loss," I said.

He just frowned and pulled out the map.

This time the map hadn't changed. My magik had worked. We were still headed for Donner, which looked to be a good distance from here. I was going to need all the energy I could get. I downed another quarter of the glass.

By the time we left the place, with me running through the same routine with the guy in the apron, promising we might be back for dinner, I had downed a glass and a half of the juice, and had the rest in the water containers. I was good to go through the night. As far as I was concerned, Tanda and Aahz could sleep while I flew. They weren't doing anything, so why not?

Later that afternoon I think they both did actually fall asleep while flashing along knee-high off the road. It was lucky for all of us I had my carrot juice.

As it happened, we were approaching another tiny little town along the road to Donner as the sun set. On the map this place wasn't even listed. It had maybe twenty buildings, all of them boarded up and shuttered. Still, Aahz figured there was no point in taking any chances, so we walked into the tiny town.

We were just about through the town when, at once, every door in the town slammed open. It was a dark and quiet night, with the sun down and the moon not yet up. That much sudden noise and movement darned near scared me right out of my skin.

"What's happening?" Tanda asked.

I didn't have a clue. From what I could tell, every person in the town, all dressed in different clothing, some in nightshirts, walked into the street like zombies, turned, and in a line headed out of town to the west.

We quickly stepped up onto the sidewalk to get out of the way as the chain of people moved past down the center of the road. There was no life in any of their eyes or fighting against what was happening to them.

"Be ready to take us back to Vortex #6," Aahz whispered to Tanda.

"Oh, I've been ready for days," she said.

The last person moved past us, leaving the town empty and every door standing wide open. I had no idea what we should do. I took the canister out of my pouch and downed the last of the second glass of carrot juice, just to be ready for whatever was coming.

Aahz motioned that we should follow them, so, moving slowly about thirty steps behind the last person, we followed the line of people out into the countryside, along the very same road we had planned on traveling.

The farther out we got, the more I expected to see the cows waiting for us, watching the zombie townspeople now. But there were no cows to be seen.

But there were a lot of naked people, yawning and stretching scattered around the fields, as if they were just waking up from a long nap.

The townspeople kept doing the zombie march as the naked people in the fields moved toward them. The first naked guy to reach the line near us grabbed an old man in a night-shirt, tipped back the old guy's head, and bit into his neck.

"Vampires," Tanda whispered.

Behind us the full moon was easing up over the edge of the hill, shining light on the feast as more and more vampires picked a meal and bit in. So this was what the round-up was all about? I couldn't believe what I was seeing.

The cows were vampires, and their feeding stock was the people. No wonder all the people in all the towns all ate vegetables and were afraid of the night. The people who lived in the towns were nothing more than cattle, being fattened for slaughter every month.

It was the cows that were the masters.

"You are not in the round-up line," a deep and pleasant voice said from behind us.

All three of us spun around as one to face two naked people. One was a man, one a woman. Their bodies were perfectly formed, their muscles toned, their eyes large and brown, like the cow's eyes along the road every night.

The woman was one of the most beautiful women I had ever seen without clothes on. No, make that *the* most beautiful. And with one glance into her eyes, I wanted to give myself to her. I didn't care if she bit me or not.

The next instant the dust storm on Vortex #6 slammed into me, snapping me out of my desire to make a fool of myself with a beautiful woman for the second time in a week.

Chapter Ten

"I can quit anytime."
S. HOLMES

The hundred slogging steps through the dust storm to the cabin seemed to get longer and longer every time I had to do it. I had no idea why we just couldn't D-Hop right into the cabin and skip all this dust and wind. I was going to ask Tanda that, as soon as things settled down.

As we got near the cabin, Tanda held up her hand for us to stop. I could barely see the dark shape of the building in the storm. There was no light in the window this time.

She did something with both arms I assumed was some sort of scanning magik that assassins knew, then motioned that it was clear and we should move forward. Therefore, Glenda wasn't here waiting for us.

I had the sudden image of one of the cow-vampires bending her over and sucking on her neck in the middle of some road somewhere. Considering what she had done to me, it was one of the nicer thoughts I had had about her in days.

We got inside and the door closed against the storm.

"Are we shielded?" Aahz asked Tanda.

"Up and solid," she said. "Skeeve was right; there is powerful energy here. I can hold the shield for as long as we need it."

"So Glenda can't pop in and surprise us?" I asked, moving to the stove to get it started before I took off my coat.

"Not a chance," Tanda said. "She hops back here, she's going to get awful dirty standing out there in the dust."

Aahz laughed. "Couldn't happen to a nicer demon."

"Want something to eat?" Tanda asked, working around in the cabinets as I sat at the table.

"Just more carrot juice," I said.

I could feel my body starting to get really tired, as if someone had pulled the energy plug and what I had left was draining onto the floor.

I dug into my pouch for the canister that I had been carrying. It was gone. I checked again and it was still not there. I couldn't remember doing anything with it, but I might have dropped it in the excitement of watching cows become vampires and bite on people.

"You have the other canister of juice?" I asked Aahz.

"Afraid not, apprentice," he said. "Left it back on Kowtow when we hopped out of there."

My first reaction was not to believe him. Then it became clear that he *had* left the rest of my carrot juice, and my reaction was anger.

"How could you do that?" I shouted.

"Easy," he said.

He showed me by reaching into his pouch, taking out an invisible canister, and dropping it to the floor.

"But what am I going to do without it?"

Again I shouted. I *needed* that carrot juice; right down to the very bottom of my soul I needed it.

"You're going to sleep for a long time," Tanda said, smiling at me.

Just her mention of sleep made me sleepy. I couldn't believe they had done this to me.

"Taking a guy's carrot juice isn't nice."

"I know," Tanda said. "But we're doing it for your own good. You haven't slept in at least three days. You need to stop moving and just lie down."

The tiredness was washing up over me like a wave on the beach. It was everything I could do to even think about saying I didn't need sleep.

How dare she tell me what I needed?

How dare Aahz leave my juice behind? Hadn't I trusted him with that juice?

"I don't need to rest," I said, my voice sounding funny to my ears.

"How about you just lie down for a few minutes and then we'll talk about it," Tanda said, helping me to me feet and moving me over to the soft-looking bed against one wall.

"Well, maybe just a minute," I said.

What could a minute hurt? I'd get back some of my energy, and then convince Tanda to hop me back to get my juice.

"Only one minute," I said.

Or at least I think I said that. I might not have, because from the moment my head touched the pillow, I don't remember another thing.

I woke up with a blinding headache and a taste in my mouth that was a cross between horse droppings and stale carrots. I rolled over and the pain hit me even harder, smashing into my head like someone was taking a hammer and pounding me right between the eyes.

"Ohhh," I said, putting both hands to my head trying to stop the agony.

"The sleeping apprentice awakes," Aahz, said, his voice far too loud for the size of the space between my ears.

"And in pain, it seems," Tanda shouted.

"Please whisper," I said, but my throat was so dry the words didn't really come out.

I wanted to die. Why hadn't they just killed me as I slept? Or maybe they had tried, which was why I hurt so much.

I also wanted to be sick, but that wasn't possible since there wasn't anything left in my stomach. But my stomach still felt like it wanted to twist inside out and come up through my throat. And the world spinning didn't help that feeling at all.

And, most of all, I really wanted to forget all the nightmares I'd had about cows turning into vampires, and the people of a dimension being nothing more than food stock. What an awful nightmare. That was the last time I had carrot juice if it caused those kind of visions.

Tanda came over and knelt beside me. I could feel her hand on my forehead, then a soft energy flowing through me, washing the pain and nausea with it. Whatever she did, it was nice.

After a moment she moved away and I opened my eyes. My head didn't hurt as much, and the world that felt as if it was smashing down on me from all sides had retreated.

I also realized that what I had thought were carrot-juice-induced nightmares had actually happened.

"That help?" Tanda asked.

I nodded, wishing I hadn't almost at once. She had taken away the pain, but the rest of the problems—upset stomach and spinning world—were still with me.

She brought me a glass of water, helping me sit up to drink it.

"Well, hangovers are sure fun, aren't they, apprentice?" Aahz asked.

"No," I managed to croak out after I took a small drink, "they are not."

"Good thing to remember next time you go bingeing."

The thought of even seeing another carrot made my stomach twist.

"Was there alcohol in the carrot juice?"

"No, but it had other stuff in it," Aahz said, "Stuff I'm guessing make the people of those towns good eating for the vampires."

My stomach twisted.

"And maybe help keep them under control," Tanda said, looking at me. "Think you can come to the table and try to eat a little something?"

"I can try," I said, "but no promises."

"Good enough. You need to eat."

"How long was I sleeping?" I asked as I stood and shuffled my way to the table.

I dropped into a chair and then tried to remain still while the world spun for a moment.

"About twelve hours," Aahz said. "We were just getting ready to head back to Kowtow when you started to wake up."

"Without me?" I asked, staring into the eyes of my mentor.

He smiled at what must have been my shocked expression.

"Just to explore and get a little closer to Donner while the vampires were back being cows. We would have left you shielded and been back in a few hours."

"You still want to see if you can get to the treasure?" I asked, not believing that Aahz would even want to go back to the place again, let alone try to get a golden-milk-giving cow that turned into a vampire.

"Sure," he said. "We're too close to turn back now."

"And just what are you going to do when you find this golden cow?"

"I asked him the same thing," Tanda said.

"I'll figure that out when we find it," Aahz said.

I nodded. "Glad I woke up then."

"I doubt you're going to be up for coming along just yet," Tanda said, putting a little sandwich and another glass of water in front of me.

"I'll be fine," I said. "Just a little carrot juice and I can fly a long ways."

The silence in the cabin was intense.

I looked at Aahz, then at Tanda and smiled. "Just kidding."

For some reason, neither of them laughed.

Along the way there were more and more cattle, bigger herds than we had seen at any other place. I was just glad that none of them were lined up along the road watching us.

The countryside was becoming pretty hilly, and the road looked like it was headed right at a fairly large mountain range. I hoped Donner was on this side of the range and not the other. My question was answered almost at once as we topped a slight ridge and could see off ahead.

I somehow managed to bring us to a stop and lower us to the ground. Considering what we were facing, I thought that was pretty good concentration.

From the top of this hill we could see Donner. It had been built going up the side of a gentle hill. From here it looked as if the buildings down low were all like the ones in the towns we had already seen, but the farther up the hill you went, the larger the buildings, the more ornate.

At the top was the palace. Only this wasn't like anything on this planet. It was made of stone and inlaid with gold that shimmered in the afternoon sun. It was like a second sun, only golden.

"Oh, my," Tanda said softly.

"No wonder there's a treasure map to this place," Aahz said. "I've never seen anything like that."

"Neither have I," Tanda said.

Well, if the two experienced dimension travelers in the group had never seen anything like the golden palace we were staring at, I sure hadn't either.

After a moment I asked what I thought was the obvious next question.

"So now what do we do?"

"We go take a closer look," Aahz said, laughing. "See what we can see."

I glanced at my mentor. He was always happy when there was a chance we might end up with a lot of money. I didn't want to ask him how he thought we were going to get any of the gold we could see from here, but clearly he had ideas, and the ideas were enough to make him smile.

All his smile did was worry me.

I flew us two more small hills closer to the city before Aahz said we had better walk the rest of the way. There was so much energy in this area that I didn't even feel tired from the effort of flying. It had come easy, which meant that all magik was easy in this place. That was both good and bad.

Ahead of us on the road were some walkers, plus a wagon full of vegetables being pulled by two horses. Cows filled the fields, paying no attention to anything.

Up closer, the town of Donner was even bigger than I had first thought, with a very wide, boulevard-like main road heading straight through everything. The golden castle on the top of the hill was massive. It looked like it could swallow the entire royal palace and courtyard of Possiltum and not even burp. I wonder if this place had a royal magician. Maybe I could apply for the job, but I doubted I would pass the cow physical.

We had just crested the last small hill and were starting down toward the edge of the city when a dozen men on horseback came galloping out of the city, kicking up a cloud of dust behind them. A few people ahead of us on the road stepped out of the way. And the wagonload of veggies had to move almost off the road and into a small ditch.

The thundering horses came on, riding hard, the men's black hats pulled down tight on their heads. I didn't have a good feeling about this, but at the same time there was no reason to think they were after us.

We moved to the side of the road as they neared, but instead of riding past, then stopped, sort of forming a circle around us, pinning us against a pasture full of cows. I clearly should have trusted my bad feeling.

"You are under arrest," a man sitting on a big black horse said. "Please come with us into the city."

"It's a posse," Tanda said, the surprise in her voice clear. "Never thought I'd ever see one."

"A what?" I asked.

"Never mind," she said.

"Under arrest for what?" Aahz demanded of the guy on the big horse.

The guy, whose face looked very similar to the guy who had been the bartender in Audry's, smiled. I didn't like the look of his little teeth at all.

"You have been charged with not complying with round-up procedures," he said, "and the unlawful use of magik."

I glanced at Aahz, then at Tanda. Now we knew for sure that this dimension knew about magik. As far as I was concerned, right about now would be a great time to beat a hasty retreat to the wonderful dust of Vortex #6. But it seemed Aahz had other ideas.

"We demand to be taken to your leader," Aahz said, stepping toward the man. "We are powerful magicians from another dimension with important information your leader will want."

The guy actually laughed, which rocked Aahz back on his heels. Not too many people actually laughed at my mentor and got away with it.

"Drop my disguise," Aahz said, whispering to me.

I shrugged. At this point, it couldn't get any worse, so I did as he asked.

Not a one of the men on the horses even seemed to notice that there was now a green-scaled ugly Pervect standing in front of them. Not even their horses cared.

That was not what Aahz was expecting.

The guy again just laughed.

"You can drop the act," he said. "Our leader knows exactly why you are here."

Then the guy did something that just flat scared me to death. He pointed a finger at Aahz and a moment later the map came floating out of Aahz's belt pouch, unfolded in mid-air, and fluttered there. Then it refolded and returned to the pouch.

"Now please come with us," he said.

He turned his horse and started at a slow pace toward the city.

I glanced at Aahz, who was looking almost stunned, then at Tanda.

"Don't you think this might be a good time to head for home?" I asked.

"I wish we could," Tanda said.

Sweat dripped off her forehead as we all stepped back onto the road to follow the guy who had done the talking. The rest of his group of riders waited and fell in behind us.

"Excuse me?" I said. "How about jumping us to the dust storm?"

"Trust me," she said, "I tried."

"You what?" I couldn't believe she couldn't get us out of this mess.

"We're blocked?" Aahz asked.

"Tighter than a vault," she said. "Best block I've ever run up against."

"How about I try to fly us out of here?"

"Won't work either," Tanda said. "At the moment there's a block over all our magik."

"Oh," was all I could say.

Ahead, just over the head of the horse in front of me, I could see the golden palace. It was the place, the treasure, we had been working and fighting so hard to reach. Right now it was the last place in any dimension I wanted to go.

Chapter Eleven

"Who are those guys?"
B. CASSIDY

No one in the city seemed to pay us any attention at all as we were marched into Donner and right up the wide Main Street of the city toward the golden palace on the hill. I saw at least a dozen Audry's-like places along the road, and this town had three guys in white hats and shovels cleaning up after the hundreds of horses. As we passed, all three of them tipped their hats and said, "Howdy."

What really made this town different from all the others we had gone through, besides the golden palace towering over it, were the pastures between the buildings. About halfway up to the palace, on the right side of the road, was a beautiful, green pasture about the size of one building.

It had one lone cow in it, grazing on the perfectly tended grass.

A little farther up the hill there were more small pastures between buildings on both sides of the street, each with just one cow. And the higher we went, the more beautiful the pastures became, with ornate decorations and well-trimmed grass.

Just under the palace were five pastures on both sides of the main boulevard, and in each of those manicured and ornately decorated lawns was one cow, and off to one side a guy wearing a white hat and carrying a shovel. Waiting. Now I knew what all the other shovel-carrying guys working the streets of all the towns were trying to advance their way up to.

The guys on horses dismounted at a massive gate made of stone pillars and gold bars. The palace itself was surrounded by a tall stone wall that looked too high to even try to climb.

The stone was highly polished and there looked to be gold lining the top.

The guy in charge pointed us at the gate, but didn't follow us in. Instead, five other men in white robes with gold trim met us just inside the gate and indicated we should follow. Each carried a golden shovel like a cane, using it to walk. It was clear that a person who worked outside the palace and didn't have a golden shovel couldn't get into the palace. Why were we so lucky?

"Would you look at all the gold!" Aahz said, his head whipping back and forth as he tried to take it all in.

"Amazing," Tananda said, her voice soft and carrying the awe she felt.

I couldn't say anything. The sight that greeted us inside that gate was beyond anything I had ever imagined. There was nothing but beautiful-trimmed lawns, gold ornaments, strangely shaped shrubs, and guys in white robes and white hats with golden shovels. Maybe a dozen different cows grazed on the beautiful lawns, clearly without a care in the world, all tended by guys in white robes with golden shovels.

Our robed jailers herded us up the stone staircase, climbing through manicured lawn after manicured lawn, all surrounded by gold statues of different animals and gold artwork. The walls of the castle itself towered over us, the white stone and shining gold walls higher than anything I had ever seen before.

We were finally taken through a big double door and headed down flights of stone steps. From there I got completely lost as we went through tunnels, down steps, around corners, down more tunnels, down more steps, all the time going deeper and farther under the castle. I didn't much like the idea of being trapped down under such a massive building, but the idea that we were being held prisoner by cows controlling guys with golden shovels bothered me even more. Especially since they were *vampire* cows.

Finally we were herded into a big room with stone walls and left, a golden-barred door slamming closed behind us. There were five others in the big room, all looking tattered and exhausted. Ten beds were spaced around the walls and all the previous prisoners were lying on the beds, sleeping.

"Glenda," Aahz said.

It took me a second to recognize the figure on the bed across the room. It was Glenda all right, but not the alive, beautiful, and powerful woman I had remembered from just a few days before. This woman wore tattered clothing, had dirt and deep circles under her eyes, and a huge red mark on her neck.

All three of us moved over to her. As we did her eyes fluttered open and she saw Aahz, then Tanda and me.

"Found the treasure, I see," she said, her voice barely a whisper.

Then she was back asleep, her breathing heavy, and her mouth hanging open. The red marks on her neck pulsed with the beat of her heart.

"I don't like the looks of this," I said.

"Any chance we can get out of here?" Aahz asked, glancing around the room.

I did the same. None of the other prisoners in the place looked to be in any better shape than Glenda. And all of them had the red marks on their necks and were sleeping heavily, almost dead.

Tanda shook her head.

"Not a chance at all. The energy is back flowing to us, but the dimension hopping is still blocked completely. I've been trying to D-hop ever since we were captured."

"Well," Aahz said, "we're just going to have to find another way out, and grab a little gold along the way."

"How about the D-Hopper?" I asked. "They didn't search us. Maybe it would work."

Aahz pulled the D-Hopper out, made sure the setting was right, then triggered it.

We stayed right where we were.

"Worth a try," I said as he put it back in his shirt.

"I think we need some answers," Aahz said.

He sat down on the edge of Glenda's bunk and then not so gently shook her awake.

"No! No!" she said as she woke.

Her hands went to her neck and then flinched away. Again it took a moment for her to recognize us. She blinked, then said, "Go away," and closed her eyes again.

"We need some answers," Aahz said.

He grabbed her by the shoulders, twisted her around, and sat her upright on the bed, her back against the wall.

"Easy there, big fella," Glenda said, her voice hoarse. "We're all in this together."

"I'm not in anything with you," Aahz said.

Looking at the wreck she had become, it was hard for me to even remember why I had been interested in her in the first place. Could I be that superficial that she had to remain beautiful for me to care? Or did I no longer find her attractive or have any interest in her because she had betrayed us? It was an interesting question I'd have to talk to Aahz about once we were safely back home.

"Oh," Glenda said, "trust me. If you're here, in this cell, then we're all in this together."

"How'd you end up here?" Aahz asked. "How'd you find the place without the map?"

She laughed. "I went to Dodge City, didn't find anything, so I asked this guy running a bar where the golden cow was, and he told me here."

I shook my head. How simple that would have been. Why hadn't we thought of it?

"Then what happened?" Tanda asked.

"Didn't even make it into town," she said. "Got picked up by a bunch of guys on horses yesterday and tossed in here. Then last night I got hauled out to be a snack at the big party upstairs."

Her hand again went to her neck and she flinched. The red marks there didn't look like they were healing very well. And I didn't much like the sound of being a snack like those people lined up on the road had been.

"It was like a bad dream," Glenda said, her eyes distant. "They kept forcing glass after glass of carrot juice down me while taking turns sucking on my neck. By morning I couldn't even walk. I don't remember how I got back down here."

The thought of carrot juice ripped my stomach into a knot.

"Who were they?" Tanda asked.

Glenda shrugged. "Hundreds of beautiful naked people in this gold-covered ballroom way up in the castle somewhere."

Aahz nodded. "Vampire cows."

"What?" Glenda asked.

"We saw a field of cows change into beautiful naked people last night," I said, "and snack on the townspeople who were waiting to be used."

She looked at me, then at Aahz. "The kid's not kidding, is he?"

Aahz shook his head.

Glenda shook her head and then closed her eyes.

"Drunk dry by bovine vampires. How ironic."

She didn't say anything else, and Aahz didn't push her. She looked as if she had lost twenty pounds in one night. She had managed to outsmart us, find her way to the castle, and still get captured. If she couldn't get away, how were we going to do it before we became a full-moon snack?

"We've got to get out of here before the sun goes down," Aahz said, standing and moving to the door.

He gave it a couple hard hits, but it didn't move, and no one came because of the noise. Clearly none of the golden-shoveled guards were worried about a prisoner escape.

"Even if we did get out," Tanda said, "it would take a map to find our way back through the castle."

"Map," I said. "That's the key."

Aahz turned and looked at me, giving me one of those I-don't-understand-how-you-can-be-so-stupid looks.

I moved over to him and stuck out my hand.

"Can I have the map, please?"

"Why would you want it?" Aahz asked.

I didn't want to tell him my idea without first seeing if I was right.

"Just give it to him," Tanda said.

Aahz shrugged and took out the map, handing it to me still folded.

I opened it up, laying it flat on the nearest empty bunk so that we could all look at it. The map looked as I had expected. It had gained its magik back once we got inside the castle. It showed where we were, fifteen levels down and under a lot of rock and gold. It also showed the room where the golden cow was, far above us.

And better yet, it showed us a path from where we were being held to what the map called a large ballroom. Clearly the map's designers had planned on continuing the game right to the very last room. It sort of made sense. Dimension to dimension until we found the right one, then town to town until we found the right one, now room to room until we found the right one. I didn't much like the game, but I understood the thinking.

"Well, would you look at that?" Aahz said, stunned.

Tanda studied the map, then looked at the wall near Glenda's bunk, then studied the map again.

It didn't take me long to see what she was doing. The map showed a way out of this room that wasn't the main door. Maybe, just maybe, we had a chance. If we could escape the cell, then avoid hundreds of men with white robes and golden shovels, and then outrun the posse on horseback, we might be able to get far enough away from the castle to dimension-hop back to Vortex #6.

It sounded impossible, but it was more than we'd had a moment ago.

I folded up the map and put it in my pouch, then headed for the wall where Glenda was still sitting on a bunk. Her eyes were closed, and if her chest hadn't been moving I would have thought she was dead.

"Wait," Tanda said as I started to get down on my knees to look for an opening in the wall under the bunk beside Glenda's, where the map indicated it would be. "We need to protect ourselves, not let anyone know what we're doing."

"And how do you suggest we do that?" I asked.

Aahz glanced around at the bunks and the blankets on them.

"Skeeve, when Tanda gives the word, I want you to make the blankets on those three bunks look like the three of us."

"Four of us," Glenda said, opening her eyes and looking clearly at Aahz. "If you've found a way to leave, I'm leaving with you."

"Yeah," Aahz said, laughing, "like you took us with you on Vortex #6? I don't think so."

"I don't go, I alert the guards," she said, staring at him. "And I've got enough power left to easily break an apprentice's disguise spell."

For a moment I thought Aahz was going to strangle her, and I wanted to help. Then Tanda stepped between them, facing Aahz.

"She's powerful and can help. Let her, or we might never get out of here."

My mentor looked like he was about to explode. He hated doing anything he didn't want to do, and taking Glenda along was something he *really* didn't want to do. But Tanda was right; maybe Glenda could help.

"All right," Aahz said, taking a deep breath and letting it slowly out.

He stepped past Tanda and looked down at Glenda.

"You work with us or we dump you faster than you dumped my apprentice in that bar. Understand?"

She nodded, clearly very weak. "Let me help Tanda with the cover spell," she said. "I'm good at them."

"I'm an ex-assassin," Tanda shot back. "I'm better."

"I know you are," Glenda said. "I can just add some depth on the cover. And help support Skeeve's disguises. We're dealing with some good magicians here. Let's make sure they don't see us coming, or leaving as the case may be."

For a moment Tanda stared at Glenda, then she nodded. "Follow my lead."

"Completely," Glenda said. She took a deep, shuddering breath and braced herself against the wall, her eyes closed.

I glanced around. The other three prisoners hadn't woken up. They looked to be in much worse shape than Glenda.

Aahz turned to me. "Get ready. On Tanda's count, one at a time, disguise the four bunks."

I took a deep breath and reached out for the energy it was going to take.

Energy here wasn't a problem. It flowed all around us like a massive river, wider and stronger than I had ever experienced. I let it flow inside me, giving me strength.

"Aahz first," Tanda said. "Now."

On the farthest empty bunk I pictured Aahz lying there, sleeping, his mouth open.

On the bunk Aahz appeared, just as I had pictured.

I gathered more energy.

"Glenda now," Tanda said.

I imagined Glenda on the second bunk, sleeping in the same way we had seen her sleeping when we came in, red mark on her neck and all.

Glenda appeared there.

"Now me," Tanda said.

I reached out and took the energy and put the image of Tanda sleeping in the next bunk

"Now you," Tanda said.

I did the same, although I had never seen myself asleep, I had an image of what I must look like, and I used that.

It was strange to see myself sleeping there. Really strange.

"All shielded," Tanda said.

Glenda nodded. "Very strong. It should hold. And good job, Skeeve."

I just nodded. I didn't need compliments from a woman who left me to rot in a town full of cow food.

"Okay, Skeeve," Tanda said, "see if you can find that opening."

I got down on my stomach and crawled partway under the bunk next to where Glenda sat. It looked like a stone wall, just like all the rest of the room. But when I went to touch the wall, my hand went through as if nothing was there.

"A disguised opening," I said.

I crawled under the bunk and right on through the wall, coming out on the other side. It was pitch black, so I tore a little piece off the bottom of my shirt and used a magik spell to light it. I was in a tunnel that had been cut out of stone. It was just tall enough for me to stand, and not much wider than my shoulders. It clearly hadn't been used in a long time, if ever. There was an unused torch stuck in a crack in the rocks, so I lit it, tossing to one side my burning piece of shirt.

A moment later Aahz followed, coming through what looked to be solid stone near the floor of the tunnel. Then Glenda, breathing hard, pulled herself into the tunnel and sat with her back against the sidewall, followed almost instantly by Tanda.

"This tunnel is shielded as well," Tanda said, looking around as she stood. "A shield so old, it might have been here before the castle."

"I'm impressed," Glenda said, still sitting on the floor. "How'd you know this was here?"

I pulled the map out of my pouch and held it up in the faint torchlight. She saw it and nodded. "Of course."

I opened the map and Aahz, Tanda, and I stood under the torch studying it.

It now showed the tunnel we were in as center, and the location of the golden cow had changed. Now it was in a dining room ten floors above us. I didn't believe it for a moment.

The map showed that we had to follow the tunnel for as far as we could, then climb up a ladder and through the floor of what was called a morgue.

"Seems we don't have much choice," Aahz said, staring at the map. He pointed to the fact that the map didn't show a way back into the room we had just left.

I moved over and touched the wall we had just crawled through. It was solid rock. Weird.

I moved back over to where they were standing under the light.

"We're going to be chasing the cow until we find an exit," Aahz said.

"We could always kill the magik in the map one more time," I said.

"No," Tanda said. "We may end up in a room that we need the map to help us get out of."

"She's right," Glenda said. "For all we know, the map may be the magik source that created this tunnel. From the looks of how that wall turned back to stone, it just might be."

I stared at the paper in my hand, then at Glenda sitting on the floor. If she was right, and I had killed the magik in the map again, we might have ended up trapped in stone. I didn't want to think about that at all.

"So we follow the magik," Aahz said.

I folded the map and put it away in my pouch, then took the torch out of the crack and held it in front of me so that I could see where I was going. Then, doing my brave routine, I started off down a tunnel so old, or so magical, that it didn't look as if anyone had ever been in here.

The tunnel sloped upward like a fairly steep ramp. I moved at a steady pace, making sure that each step was on solid ground. I didn't trust my eyes at this point, after crawling through solid rock.

After about a hundred paces I looked back. Tanda was right behind me, Aahz behind her, and Glenda was managing to stay up with us, only because I was moving so slowly. I didn't feel the slightest bit sorry for her. She had left me to die, and gotten herself into the mess she faced last night. And without us, she wouldn't have this chance to escape. As far as I was concerned, she would either keep up or go out on her own again.

I went back to working my way up the tunnel, testing each step, until finally I reached the end. A rock ladder had been carved into the stone, leading straight up through a very narrow hole.

As Aahz stopped beside me I pointed up at the hole.

"Can you squeeze through there?"

"Do I have a choice?"

"I suppose not," I said. I handed him the torch. "Let me get up through the opening so I can brace my back against the wall, then hand me the torch."

Without waiting for another idea from my mentor, I started up. The hole in the roof of the tunnel was big enough that my shoulders touched on both sides, but not so small that I had to squeeze. Aahz might be able to make it, but it was going to take some work.

Once I got through the hole, the space got bigger. I stopped and Aahz handed me the torch, passing it up past me quickly so I wouldn't get burned.

Above I could see the ladder climbing at least twenty or so of my body lengths before reaching what looked to be a wooden trapdoor in a floor.

"Send Tanda up second," I whispered down to Aahz below me. "We need to make sure no one is in the room above the trap door up here."

"Good thinking," Tanda said, climbing up under me as I went higher. She got up just under me, paused, and then nodded. "No one up there at the moment."

"Good," I said.

"You go next," I heard Aahz say to Glenda down in the tunnel.

"No," Glenda said, her voice firm. "You get stuck in that opening it's going to take both Tanda pulling and me shoving to get you through."

I couldn't hear what Aahz said, but a moment later his green-scaled head came through the hole below Tanda.

"No, both arms ahead of you," Tanda said.

Aahz backed down a step, put both his arms over his head, and climbed back up into the hole. From what I could see, his shoulders were wedged pretty good in the rock.

Tanda braced herself, grabbed one of his hands, and then said, "Ready to push, Glenda?"

"Ready," Glenda said, her voice muffled as if she were a long ways away.

"Now," Tanda said, pulling on Aahz's arm as he pulled on the rock surface with the other.

With a rip of his shirt, he came through.

Tanda let go and moved up under me. Aahz had his shoulders through the hole, but he wasn't climbing any higher at the moment.

"Glenda," he said. "Grab a hold of my leg and I'll pull you up."

"I think I can make it," she said.

"Just do it and quit arguing with me," Aahz said.

I stared down at the top of my mentor's head. The old green-scaled guy had a soft spot after all. Always knew it was there, just hadn't seen it that often.

As Aahz helped Glenda up the stone ladder, Tanda and I went on up to the trap door. Since Aahz hadn't taught me a spell yet that could sense if something was on the other side of a wall, or a floor in this case, I was leaving that up to Tanda.

"We still in the clear?" I asked.

"We are," Tanda said.

I eased up to the wooden trapdoor and pushed slowly. The wood scraped as it went up, then the door seemed to catch on something. It took me a moment to realize it was a rug. From the looks of it, a very old rug.

I pushed even harder, and the rug lifted and pulled aside enough so that I could get through. I went halfway up through the trapdoor and stood, torch in the air, lighting the dark room.

Tanda had been right. From what I could see, no one was around. Just a bunch of tables and a wooden door leading off to the left. But the minute I stepped up and stood, I knew that Tanda and I had both been wrong. No one *alive* was around.

But the place was filled with dead people. Tables full of them.

Chapter Twelve

"There's gotta be a way out of this dungeon."
G. GYGAX

Okay, this was another first for me. I had never had the luck, opportunity, or bad timing to be in a room full of dead people. And these weren't just *any* dead people, but people who had clearly had the life sucked out of them through their necks just the night before. There had to be at least fifteen or twenty bodies, all naked, with ugly marks on their necks, and eyes staring at the ceiling.

I stood, holding the torch in the air, not really wanting to move in any direction until the others were beside me. Not that I thought the dead could do anything to me, or that I was superstitious about dead spirits. I wasn't, I was sure. I just didn't want to make a wrong move until I had someone beside me, or at least that was what I told myself.

"Looks like you were lucky to survive last night," Aahz said to Glenda as helped her through the trap door and onto her feet.

"Does seem that way, doesn't it," she said, leaning against a table with a dead guy on it.

The guy looked a lot like the guy who ran Audry's. I was starting to think that most of the men on this planet looked like him.

"So much for thinking they didn't kill their food source," Tanda said.

"I don't think most do," Aahz said. "But this is the castle, the royalty of the planet. I would imagine in here all rules are off."

"Wonderful," I said. "Now we have naked killer vampire cows, one of which is rumored to give golden milk."

"Strange place, isn't it?" Aahz said.

"You could say that, but you just did."

"We need to put that rug back and close the trap," Tanda said. "Make sure we cover our tracks as best we can."

I handed Tanda the torch and Aahz and I sat to work. In a few seconds the room looked like it had before we came up out of the floor.

"Now where?" Glenda asked.

I pulled out the map and opened it, holding it up to the light for Aahz and Tanda to see. The morgue, the room we were in, was now central on the map. The golden cow had moved to the kitchen. And our path out of here was through a panel in the back of the room, not the door. The map showed the panel leading to a secret passageway that led for a long ways up through the castle.

"You know," I said, pointing at where the passageway led, "that we are getting deeper and deeper into the castle and farther from an escape exit."

"Looks that way, doesn't it?" Aahz said, staring at the map.

"That doesn't matter and you know it, Aahz," Glenda said. "At least you could tell your apprentice the truth."

We all turned and looked at where she was leaning on a table with a naked dead guy right behind her.

"How's that?" Aahz asked, clearly not happy at Glenda's tone.

"We can't escape this place without beating this map," she said. "And beating the map means capturing the golden cow, who I assume, is the leader of this entire dimension. That golden cow is the only one who is going to let us go, and you know it."

At that point I was convinced that all the blood loss had gotten to her mind. The only thing I wanted to do was find a way out and run or fly as fast as we could until we were far enough away that we could hop dimensions and get away from this insane place.

"Come on," I said, smiling at her. "That would be crazy. Going after the head of all the cow vampires would be suicide. We'd end up like all these fine food products around us. Glenda, it's clear you need to rest."

No one said anything. Glenda just kept staring at me and slowly I realized that neither Aahz or Tanda were telling her how crazy she was either.

I turned to my mentor, who had a sheepish look on his face.

"She's right," he said. "We wouldn't stand a chance of getting out of here, against the kind of magik we are facing, without the help of the map."

I looked at Tanda.

She smiled at me. "They're right. I can barely, with Glenda's assistance, keep us hidden. The magik around here is so powerful, we wouldn't stand a chance without help from the top. And the map is leading us to that help."

At that moment I knew, without a shadow of a doubt, that I was as dead as any of the bodies in the room with us. I just wasn't smart enough yet to lie down and stop breathing like they had all done.

With one more look at my mentor, then at Glenda, I shrugged and tried to put on my best death-mask face.

"Why not? Let's get moving before someone comes in and stops our fun treasure hunt before it really gets started."

With one more look at the map, I folded it and put it back in my pouch.

Then I headed through the tables of bodies to the back wall. As I went I wanted to talk to the bodies, tell them I'd be right back, tell them to wait, to reserve a table for me. But I kept my morbid thoughts to myself.

There was a large cabinet of medical supplies filling the back wall and no hidden panel that I could see. From what the map had shown, the panel was right behind the cabinet.

I took hold of the back edge of the cabinet and pulled outward. I expected it to be too heavy for me to move, but it swung easily and silently, opening up into a passageway behind the panel.

I glanced back at Tanda and Aahz and Glenda, who were silently watching me.

"Give me the torch and follow me," I said. "We'll check the map again when we get a ways inside. And pull this closed behind you."

Aahz nodded.

It felt good to be leading, even if I wasn't going in a direction I wanted to go. At least I'd get to the wrong place first, and more than likely be killed first.

Tanda handed me the torch and I slipped behind the cabinet.

The passageway was as wide as a small hallway back in the Possiltum palace. It was mostly made of wood, with some stone walls along the way. Unlike the passageway cut out of the rock below the morgue, this looked like it had had regular traffic over the years.

I stayed in the faint path in the dust and moved ten steps down the secret passageway, then stopped. Aahz pulled the cabinet closed and motioned that he was ready. I wondered if we could go back that way if we had to, but I didn't want Aahz to check, simply for the fear of finding out we couldn't.

About a hundred paces along the secret passageway branched into two. One went to the right and up slightly, while the other went seemingly straight as far as the light from our torch would show.

Tanda was behind me and I handed her the light, again pulling out the map.

It had changed again, showing the passageway we were in and the intersection. The map now wanted us to go right. And up.

I remembered being in front of this castle and looking up as it towered over us. I had never seen anything so big before. Now it seemed that if this map had its way, which Aahz and Tanda were determined to give it, we would end up at the top.

Maybe up there I'd have a good view when all the life was sucked out of me.

The passageway sloped upwards, sometimes stairs, sometimes just a ramp. It bent to the right, then in twenty paces to the right again, as if going around a room. From that point on it just kept turning and twisting and climbing. After twenty minutes I was so turned around and lost, I couldn't even begin to tell you what part of the castle we were in. All I knew was that we had gone up a great deal. Finally the corridor ended at the top of a short flight of stairs.

I stopped and waited as Tanda caught up. Then, ten steps behind her, came Aahz helping Glenda. He sure was being nice, for some reason, to a woman who had betrayed him. That wasn't like Aahz at all. Clearly he needed her for something, and I was never far enough away from Glenda to ask what it was.

When they caught up, Glenda slumped to the ground and closed her eyes and I pulled out the map and looked at where it was taking us. It showed the end of the secret passageway where we were standing, and a secret door into a giant ballroom was right in front of me. I glanced at the wall. I couldn't see where it was, but I assumed that when I needed it, it would be there.

I went back to studying the map again. We had to go into the ballroom and to the far wall where there was another panel into another passageway. The golden cow treasure was now marked as being in the throne room a number of floors above us.

"Looks like we get to go out in the open for the first time," Aahz said, studying the map.

"There's no one out there at the moment," Tanda said.

"So we need to do it and quickly," I said, folding up the map.

"Keep the map handy," Aahz said. "When we get into the ballroom, you need to check it again."

"Of course," I said, nodding and acting as if I had known that, even though I hadn't yet thought of it.

"Can you make it a little farther, Glenda?" Aahz asked.

Glenda jerked and pushed herself to her feet, leaning against the wall.

"I can make it as far as I need to make it."

Aahz just nodded. "Then let's go."

Tanda had the torch, so I went to the wall and pushed where the secret panel was supposed to be and surprise,

surprise, the wall opened. I slid through. At first I thought there was nothing on the other side of the panel, that the map had lied to us. Then I realized that the secret door was pushing out a massive drape or tapestry of some type.

I ducked to the right under the cloth and out into the open, with Tanda and the torch right behind me.

At the moment we didn't need the light. The room had massive, two-story-high windows along one side that let in the natural sunlight. The hills in the distance were like old friends calling to me. I so much wanted to be out there instead of in here. The sun, from what I could tell, was within an hour of setting on the other side of the castle. We needed to pick up speed if we were going to find the golden cow before it became the golden vampire.

"Wow," Tanda said, looking around at the gold-inlaid panels and golden ceilings of the massive ballroom.

The floor was a highly polished white stone with streaks of gold running through it. In my wildest imaginings I could have never come up with a ballroom as fancy or beautiful as this one.

Aahz and Glenda stopped beside us in the huge room. I bet at least five hundred people could've danced in this room without even bumping into one another.

"I remember being in this room last night," Glenda said softly.

The thought of her being here with a bunch of naked vampires chewing on her neck made me shudder.

"Then let's not wait for the music to start," I said.

I opened up the map and looked at it. Again, just coming through the secret door had caused the map to change. Now the way out of here wasn't across the room, but up on what looked like a stage near the back of the room, directly across from the windows.

"This way," I said, leading the way up a short staircase and onto a massive wooden stage.

On the back wall was nothing but wood slats. I glanced at the still-open map in my hand, then moved to what looked to be about the right area, putting the map back into my pouch as

I went. After just a few seconds of trying, I found the loose boards, pulled them aside, and we were back out of the light and into what I thought was another dark passageway.

Tanda came in behind me, holding the torch up so that we could both see what was ahead.

I froze like a statue at what I saw.

"Well I'll be a grave-digger's monkey," Tanda said.

Ahead of us wasn't another passageway, but a massive, low-ceilinged room. Rows and rows and rows of shelves lined the walls, and down the middle of the room, side-by-side, packed close on every inch of every shelf, were skulls.

Cow skulls.

Thousands and thousands and thousands of white, empty-eyed cow skulls.

Aahz finished making sure the slats were back in place behind us, then turned and stopped cold beside me. I was glad to see he had the same reaction I did. It was always good to know my mentor could be shocked.

"Someone want to explain this to me?" Glenda asked, her voice echoing through the remains of an entire herd.

"Maybe it's a thousand years of former royal family?" Aahz said. "Look at that one."

He pointed at one skull hung on the wall, ornately decorated with gems.

I knew that wasn't exactly right. I could feel it in the energy in this place. After a moment I turned to Tanda.

"Can you feel anything odd in here?"

"Power," she said.

"An energy focus?" Aahz asked.

"Sure seems that way," Tanda said. "Or maybe there's something special about these skulls, something in them that magnifies the magikal power of this area and turns it into something different."

I found myself, to my own amazement, moving forward toward the closest shelf of skulls. I reached out and lightly touched the smooth, cool surface of one. It did have energy, but not energy like I had been taught by Aahz to use. There was different energy in it, used for something more than just magik.

"Vampire energy," I said.

Tanda and Glenda came up beside me, each carefully reaching out and touching a skull.

"He's right," Tanda said. "These skulls seem to take magical energy and change it, radiating the new energy needed to turn cows into vampires."

"Are you kidding me?" Aahz asked, standing off to one side.

"No, she's not," Glenda said. She waved her hand at the thousands and thousands of skulls. "Welcome to the energy source of the vampire rulers of this world."

"And the energy is starting to get stronger," Tanda said. "I can feel it."

"The sun is going down," I said. "We need to get out of here."

I opened up the map and looked at it. Through the room, against the far wall, was the door we needed to go through. And on the other side of that door was something I hadn't expected us to get so close to this fast.

The golden cow.

The treasure we had come so far to find. It was one secret door away, in a room called the Meadow.

"Take a look at this," I said, spreading the map out for everyone to see.

"Now what do we do?"

Aahz looked at the map and smiled.

"We go capture us a leader as a hostage and make sure we get our freedom."

"Sounds good to me," Tanda said.

"Why don't I think it's going to be that easy?" I said.

"Because it never is." Glenda said.

Around me the empty-eyed cow skulls started to hum faintly and vibrate a little, filling the room with a noise that ate at my very soul.

"Whatever we're going to do," Tanda said, her hands over her ears, "let's do it fast."

Again I stuffed the map in my pouch and, with my hands over my ears as well, I headed through the middle of thousands of humming skulls toward the secret panel in the far wall.

By the time I got there the sound from the skulls in my head was so painful I didn't even stop. I just went right on through and out onto a thick carpet of beautiful grass.

Aahz, Tanda, and Glenda followed me, with Aahz shutting the secret panel behind us, instantly stopping the painful energy pounding at my head. I would have been relieved if I hadn't been so stunned at what faced me.

There was a guy, sitting in a lounge chair on the other side of the field of grass, reading a newspaper. If he had had on a white apron, he would have looked almost exactly like the guy who had waited on us in Audry's.

The setting sun was pouring through one of the room's giant windows and turning the nearby hills to a wonderful shade of gold and pink and red.

I glanced around. Except for the patch of grass we were standing on, the room looked like a large suite, with a big bed, a kitchen against one wall, and a private bathroom area off to one side.

The guy was sitting in what looked like a livingroom area, except that there was only one chair. He looked over at us, then shook his head as if not believing what he was seeing. Then he looked at us again and jumped to his feet, an expression of sheer joy and happiness on his face.

"My wonderful heavens!" he shouted. "You've finally come!"

"I think he's happy to see us," Tanda whispered.

The guy came toward us, his face almost breaking from the smile filling it.

"Really happy," I whispered back.

"My friends, my friends, come in," he said, motioning us to come toward his living area. "Don't be afraid. I'm just so happy you have arrived."

"You are?" Aahz asked.

The guy laughed.

"I am. I honestly am. I can't believe after all this time the map has finally brought someone to rescue me!"

Chapter Thirteen

"You can't always get what you want."
M. JAGGER

The guy led us off the grass and into what was clearly his home.

"Sorry for the mess," he said, scampering about picking up a book here, a notebook there, some dishes which he quickly put in the sink. We all just sort of stood in a group watching him. "My name is Harold. I'm sorry I don't have enough chairs for you all."

He looked like a Harold. The name fit him, and all the other guys who looked a lot like him in all the Audry's-like places we had been in. Harold pulled his one kitchen chair away from the small table and set it out, then indicated that one of us should take it and another should take his recliner. It was beyond clear that he never got guests of any kind—at least the type of guests he wanted to sit down with. I think at that point we were all so stunned by what he had said, we really weren't reacting well. I know I wasn't. I have no real idea what I thought I was going to find when we got to the "treasure," but a guy waiting to be rescued sure wasn't it. And a guy who had used the map to bring his rescuers would have never occurred to me. Only Glenda took his offer of the recliner and settled into it with a deep sigh. The guy looked at her, worried.

"You were captured and taken last night, were you not?"

"I was," she said.

Harold looked sincerely upset. "I'm so sorry. You're so lucky you survived it."

"We saw a room full of people who didn't," Aahz said.

The poor guy looked like he might just faint away right there. He was wringing his hands, shaking his head, and pacing.

"It's all my fault, you know. All my fault."

"Okay," Aahz said, trying to calm the guy a little. "You want to explain to us what's going on?"

"Actually start from the beginning," I said, leaning against the kitchen counter.

From where I stood I could see out the two-story-tall windows that flanked one side of the big room. The valley below was in complete shadow, but the sun still covered the mountains and streamed in through the window onto the grass. If this was a prison, it was the nicest jail cell I had seen in a long time.

Harold nodded. "I'm sorry, I am just so shocked you are here, that the map worked."

"The beginning," Aahz reminded him.

"Please?" Tanda said. "Right now you are looking at four of the most confused people you have ever seen."

"Okay," Harold said, his head nodding like it was on a spring. He glanced at the window and then took a deep breath. "I've only got a half-hour until sunset and this is a long story. I might have to continue it in the morning."

"No problem," Aahz said, clearly doing his green-scaled best to calm the guy. "Just start and we'll go from there."

Again Harold did the nodding routine, his head going up and down so hard I was sure he was going to have a neck ache. "First off, you're standing in what centuries ago used to be called Count Bovine's Castle."

Okay, I have to say that I wasn't the one who started the snickering. Tanda was, with her snort. Then Aahz started shaking his head, clearly trying to contain himself, and I just couldn't keep the laugh inside anymore. Thank heavens the guy was so lost in trying to tell us the story he didn't notice.

"For as long as history recorded," Harold said, gathering speed on his tale, "Bovine's type and our people lived in an uneasy balance. They fed off of us; we killed them when we discovered them. Everything was in balance. The legends go that Count Bovine, a very long-lived and smart vampire, found this area and took it over. He enslaved the people of Donner and built this castle."

Harold waved his arms in both directions to make sure, I guess, that we knew he meant the castle we were sitting in.

"Then Count Bovine led his people in a revolt against my people, using the power that came from this castle. Over a period of a hundred years he swept out over everything and was on the verge of wiping my kind from the face of this planet."

The guy glanced at the window. The sun was on the tops of the mountains. Sunset was close.

Harold went on. "Of course, during that time Bovine's people also wiped out almost all other living creatures here as well with their blood thirsty ways. Day in and day out, they just couldn't get enough blood to satisfy themselves."

It suddenly dawned on me, that except for horses, we hadn't seen any other creatures since we had gotten here. No dogs or wild animals. Nothing but cows, horses, and people.

"Okay, a quick question," I said. Harold nodded with a glance at the window. "You're saying that Bovine's people were not cows at that point, but were people like you, just vampires?"

"Yes," Harold said. "In fact, it is rumored that vampires originally came from our species, but that fact is lost in time, if true."

"It's that way on other dimensions," Aahz said. "so it is more than likely it was that way here as well."

Harold nodded. "I had heard that as well."

"So what happened?" I asked.

"Count Bovine, who was not a stupid individual, understood that something had to be changed or his people would wipe out my people, who were his people's only remaining food source."

"Makes sense," Tanda said. "You lose your food, you die as well."

"Exactly," Harold said. "So he struck a deal with the few remaining of my people to take his people away for all but the nights of the full moon, if my people would serve his kind during that time as food."

"And your people agreed?" Glenda asked, sounding as stunned as I was feeling.

"I don't think my ancestors had a choice," Harold said. "Using the magik of this area, Count Bovine put a spell on the rest of my people. Then, using an even more powerful magik spell, he changed his people to cows."

"So while they were cows," Aahz asked, "why didn't your people just kill them all? Seems like it would have been easy."

"It would have been," Harold said, "if not for the magik that keeps us from doing just that, and keeps us from advancing. The magik allows us to do nothing but prepare for the round-up. Month in and month out, for centuries now, we have done nothing else." Harold just shook his head and went on. "Bovine's people became contented cows, careful how they treated us during the full-moon nights when they regained their normal form and had parties. We became the feed animals, content to do nothing but prepare constantly to serve our cow masters. It was survival for us, but not much of one."

Harold glanced once more out the window. The sun was just a minute from leaving the top of the distant mountaintop. "Quickly, follow me," he said, moving toward the bathroom area of his living quarters.

"What happens now?" Tanda asked.

"I become a cow for the night, the vampires roam the castle feeding and killing like the history says happened, and if you don't hide in a magically protected area, they will find you."

I was right behind him when Harold led us into his bathroom, opened a cabinet on the wall, touched a place inside the cabinet, and stepped back as a wall behind a toilet started moving inwards.

"This is the most magically protected room in all the castle," Harold said. "Stay in there until I open the door. Under no circumstances come out. Understand?"

"We understand," Aahz said.

I was the first one through the door, with Tanda and Glenda right behind me. Aahz took a moment longer, talking about something with Harold for a moment, then he joined us.

Behind the wall the space had been carved out of solid stone that was streaked in gold. It was warm and lit by the golden glow of the gold from the walls. The entire room was filled with old books, scrolls, desks, chairs, and more antiques than I had ever seen in one place. We were all inside when the guy slid the wall panel closed behind us without another word.

"Not even a wave goodnight," Tanda said.

Glenda moved inside and right to an antique couch against one wall.

"If you don't mind," she said, lying down and closing her eyes. "I think I need a nap."

"Good idea," Aahz said. Then he looked at me and held up a gold-threaded rope that he had gotten somewhere. He put his finger to his mouth to indicate that we should all be quiet. Then he moved over and took an old blanket from another antique.

"I got a blanket here to cover you," Aahz said to Glenda. "Keep you warm for the night."

"Thanks," Glenda murmured, clearly almost asleep.

Aahz moved over to her, motioning for Tanda and me to follow silently. I had no idea what he wanted me to do. Aahz put the blanket over her, wrapping the rope over her as well. Smooth move. She would never know it was there.

He pointed that I should pull the end of the rope that had dropped down against the wall under the couch.

I got on my knees and did just that, then gave the end to him as Aahz pretended to tuck the blanket around her. With a quick knot he tied the rope and stepped back.

Tanda and I both stepped back with him. I didn't know how one loop would hold someone like Glenda, or why she even needed to be held. But clearly Aahz had known something I hadn't, which was normal.

Glenda started thrashing, back and forth, back and forth, clearly trying to get out of the bind, yet the golden rope never seemed to tighten or strain in holding her. Then her eyes opened as if seeing a terror I sure didn't want to see.

"What's happening?" I whispered.

Aahz motioned for me to be silent as Glenda's mouth opened into a scream that never really came. Her back arched her up against the blanket and rope, and she held that pose for a good thirty seconds.

It was the longest thirty seconds I had experienced. I couldn't take my eyes off of her and the look of pure terror on her face. Then whatever she was going through was over. She slumped back, closed her eyes, and began to snore.

Aahz motioned that we should move away through the books and old papers and scrolls.

"Okay, what just happened there?" Tanda asked a half-second before I asked the same question.

"Harold gave me the rope to save her from becoming a vampire," Aahz said. "It seems that those left alive last night were the ones they liked."

"So that was why Glenda's body wasn't in that morgue with the others," I said.

"Exactly," Aahz said. "They were trying to turn her, have her join them."

I glanced back at where Glenda was snoring. "So she's not going to be a vampire now?"

Aahz shrugged. "We'll keep the rope on her until morning just to make sure."

"How about for two days?" Tananda asked.

Aahz laughed and said, "Maybe."

As far as I was concerned, we could keep the rope on her for the next month. When it came to Glenda, my motto was *better safe than sorry*.

Spending the night trapped in the middle of a culture's entire history, afraid that at any moment I might get taken and have my blood sucked, is an experience I would not wish on my worst enemy. The room we were trapped in was huge, with a high, domed ceiling and row after row of shelves full of old books alternating with piles of ancient furniture. Unlike Aahz and Tanda, I was not the scrounge-through-old-things kind of person. Old stuff was dusty and usually boring, as far as I was concerned. I thumbed through a few books and blew the dust off some old scrolls that looked like cookbooks. I decided I didn't want to know what they were trying to tell me about how to cook, so I wandered over to another aisle, found an antique couch tucked off to one side of a pile of furniture, managed to get most of the dust off of it, and lay down.

Tanda and Aahz were reading, whispering to each other about their finds, clearly excited about what they were seeing. I was beyond being excited about anything at this point. I was just tired. Yet for some strange reason (namely vampire cows and fear of getting my blood drained and ending up naked on a metal table in a morgue), I couldn't get to sleep. Instead I lay there, finally turning onto my back and staring at the high ceiling.

Maybe an hour into the attempt at sleep, it finally dawned on me what I was looking at every time I opened my eyes. On the smooth, stone ceiling surface someone had painted something a long, long time ago. Now, in the weird light from the glowing walls, and all the dust of the years, it was faded and almost invisible. But it was still there.

And the more I lay on my back staring at it, the more I realized that what I was seeing was the most important thing in the room as far as we were concerned. It was a map of the entire castle, only it wasn't a map of the current castle, but the layout of Count Bovine's castle.

The more I studied the drawing, the more I could see in the faint outlines. I found Harold's living area, which at one point must have been Bovine's royal suite.

The room we were now in was shown as a private library. And the skull room was there as well, labeled as "royal storage." But what was really interesting was the passageway that led from this room down into the mountain, away from the Royal Suite, down to a point that seemed to show an energy focal point of some sort in a large room. The energy point was drawn on the very center of the dome, which I also found interesting.

After another hour I was sure I had the important areas of the map pretty well memorized, including some escape routes from the castle I didn't think any vampire cow would know about.

I stood and moved over to where Aahz and Tanda were sitting at desks pouring over books. Glenda was still asleep on her couch, the golden rope tied around her.

"Have a good nap?" Aahz asked.

"A productive one," I said.

He looked at me with his normal puzzled frown and then pointed at the book he had open in front of him.

"Says here that this area around the castle is the magik focal area of the entire dimension. Before Count Bovine took it over, it was a spa area where demons from all the dimensions nearby came to soak up the concentrated magik forces and become rejuvenated."

"Powerful stuff," I said.

"More than anything I've seen before," Aahz said.

Tanda pointed at what she had been reading. "This book says that the war between the vampires and the normal folks lasted for over two hundred years and killed almost everything. This was one of the last books put in here before the exodus."

"Exodus?" I asked.

Aahz nodded. "It seems, from what we can gather, that when the compromise was reached to save both sides, Count Bovine and his people left this area, this castle, putting a shield up around it to keep everyone out of the magik."

"It seems the count didn't trust his own people with this kind of power," Tanda said.

"So what became of this count?" I asked.

Aahz shrugged. "Maybe Harold will tell us in the morning."

"Well, before that I've got something to show you."

I had them follow me back to my couch.

"I really don't feel like a nap," Aahz said.

"Just trust me," I said, pointing to a pile of furniture ten paces away. "Pull that other couch over here."

He shook his head, but did as I suggested.

"Now both of you lie on that couch," I said, dropping onto the one I had been on for hours earlier. "And lie on your backs."

Neither of them moved, and both looked annoyed. "What, can't trust me for five seconds?" I asked, smiling up at them.

Aahz snorted and then lay down, scooting over enough to give Tanda a little room as well.

I pointed upward. "What do you see?"

"A dark ceiling and a lot of dust," Tanda said.

"I see myself wasting my time," Aahz said. "There's a lot of information here that we need to—"

Silence filled the old library. After a few long seconds I said, "Interesting, isn't it?"

"What?" Tanda demanded. "Would you stop playing games and just tell me what is going on?"

To me the map was now as clear as if it were printed on a white piece of parchment. "It's a drawing," I said, pointing to the clearest lines to Tanda's right.

"It's a map," Aahz said.

"Exactly," I said. "And if you study it long enough, you can see where we are."

"Oh, my heavens," Tanda said to herself, now clearly seeing the drawing of the castle.

"After a few minutes of looking at it, the lines become clearer," I said. "Take a look to the right of the room we're in."

I didn't say anything else, giving them both time to study what I had been looking at for hours. Then finally Aahz said, "It looks like there's a corridor there."

"Where?" Tanda demanded.

"Off the room shown as a private library," I said. "On the opposite side from the royal suite."

"And it leads downward," Aahz said.

"To this area's power," I said. "Do you have any idea what standing in the middle of that kind of energy focal point would feel like?"

Both Tanda and Aahz looked at me.

"Like nothing you could ever imagine, apprentice," Aahz said.

"True," Tanda said, going back to staring at the drawings on the ceiling. "but Skeeve might be the only one who can go down there."

"I know," Aahz said, also going back to studying the roof over his head.

"Exactly what do you mean by that?" I asked, not liking the idea that I might have to take that old corridor alone into the middle of the mountain.

Aahz sighed. "I've lost my powers; Tanda is an assassin, not a magician, and we can't trust Glenda. You're it, apprentice. If one of us has to go down there, it has to be you."

I stared at the roof, following the ancient corridor down into the center of the mountain to a place of unimaginable power. For the moment, the idea of getting my blood sucked by a vampire cow didn't seem so bad.

Chapter Fourteen

"Things are looking up."
MICHELANGELO

The rest of the night just crawled past. Aahz and Tanda stayed on the couches with me for the longest time, studying the map and trying to figure out how we were going to get out of here. I noticed that, once Aahz discovered there was no golden cow, and that the map had been a sham to get someone to save Harold, he became very interested in just leaving. I supposed that was better late then never.

Aahz was sitting at one of the desks while Tanda and I stood beside him when the wall opened up and Harold stepped in. Through the opening I could see daylight flooding into the main area beyond the bathroom. It seemed we had survived another full-moon night in the land of cow vampires.

Harold stepped in and glanced at where Glenda was still sleeping. She hadn't moved at all during the night.

"Did she try to get away?" Harold asked.

"Only when the sun went down, and only for a few seconds," Aahz said. "The rope held her."

"Then she's safe," Harold said.

"What did the rope do?" I asked, not really clear on the concept that a simple rope like that could hold even a child, let alone a person who wanted to be a vampire.

"Basically, the magik in the rope stopped her from changing," Harold said. "And leaving it on her all night cleaned her system of any chance of it ever happening. Check her neck if you want to make sure."

I moved over to Glenda. Drool had run out of her mouth and formed a wet spot on the blanket. And she was snoring lightly. I put a finger on her temple and eased her head over so I could see the vampire bite marks on her neck. Where her skin had been red and inflamed, it had now returned to normal. Only a few faint marks that looked more like freckles were left of the infection.

"Amazing," I said.

Aahz had moved up behind me. "It sure is."

"Leave the rope on her for a while longer and let her sleep," Harold said. "It will do her good, give her body time to replace the blood drained from it."

I glanced at Glenda again. For a moment I almost felt sorry for her. Almost. Then I remembered she had stranded me in this world with no thought of ever coming back for me, and the feeling-sorry emotion left quickly.

"So how did you survive the night?" Tanda asked.

Harold just shrugged. "The same way I have survived every full-moon night for more years than I want to think about. I turned into a cow, ate grass, and slept standing up."

"Oh," Tanda said. "You going to explain that to us in the rest of your story?"

Harold laughed. "It's a part of it." Then he looked around. "This is a pretty amazing room, isn't it?"

"It is," Aahz said. "We learned some interesting history from some of these books."

I noticed that Aahz didn't say anything about the ceiling map, and I sure wasn't going to either. I wondered if Harold even knew about it.

"Good," Harold said. "That will give you some more background on what happened with me, and how we got like this. Shall we go back out into the sunlight?"

"What about her?" I asked, motioning toward the sleeping Glenda.

Harold shrugged. "She won't wake up as long as the rope is on her. She'll be fine right there."

We followed him out into the main room. It felt great to see light again. Spending the night in a dusty room worrying about what might happen at any moment wasn't my ideal evening.

"Anyone like something to eat?" he asked, moving into the kitchen area. We stood around the counter, watching him.

"Anything but carrot juice," Aahz said, smiling at me.

"Not funny," I said.

Harold looked at both of us and shrugged, clearly having no idea what we were talking about. "I can make you a horse-steak sandwich, a cucumber sandwich, or a salad with fresh tomatoes. And I've got either orange juice or water to drink."

"Wow, you eat better than the rest of your people," Tanda said.

"I do?" he asked, surprised. "It's been so long since I've been out of these rooms, I wouldn't know."

"A lot better," I said. "but at the moment I'd just like a glass of water."

Aahz and Tanda agreed and as he got the water Aahz prompted him to start his story again. "You got up to the point where your people and Count Bovine's people had come to an agreement, his people were changed to cows for most of the month, and this place was sealed off. What changed?"

"Actually," Harold said, "I changed it."

"Why?" Aahz asked, a fraction of a second before I could.

"Because I thought I knew better, knew what was best for my people, knew how to change things back to a better world."

"Better back up and tell us how that kind of thinking got started," Tanda said.

Harold nodded. "I met a dimension traveler named Leila. I was running this little restaurant and bar just down the road from here when Leila walked in. We got talking, she told me about the big world outside of this dimension, and then offered to let me be her apprentice. She said I had great magical potential."

I glanced at Aahz, who ignored me. Not once had Aahz ever said I had great magical potential, and I certainly wasn't going to ask him if I did. He'd just say no and laugh. Mostly laugh.

"Leila took me dimension-hopping with her, showed me hundreds of different places, taught me some basics of magik, then got killed by an assassin."

I could tell from the look in Harold's eyes that even though that had been some time ago, he still missed her. And might even have been in love with her.

"So after she was killed I got a D-Hopper and came back here. The magik block over this old castle was pretty basic, intended to just keep Count Bovine and my people out. But I had been trained in some magik, so I got in, knocking the block down.

"A little knowledge can be dangerous," Aahz said, glancing at me.

It was my turn to ignore him.

"It sure can be," Harold said. "I sat up house right here and found the room you stayed in last night, and started learning about what had happened to my people. And the more I read, the more convinced I became to try to save my people and wipe out the vampires once and for all."

"In other words," Tanda said, "you started the war again."

Harold nodded at Tanda's blunt statement. "Basically, I did. Yes."

"So what went wrong?" Aahz asked.

"Count Bovine came back," Harold said.

"What?" I said. "How could he? He'd have to be thousands and thousands of years old."

"He is," Harold said.

Aahz stared at me. "When are you going to get it through your head that powerful vampires, like powerful magicians, live a very long time?"

"Okay, okay," I said. "Go on with your story."

"I actually didn't know that Count Bovine could be alive either," Harold said. "Since I was free from the magical spell that kept the cows safe, I started gathering up help. One by one, I gathered a gang, broke the spell over them, and started planning. When there were about fifty of us, all trained and on horseback, we set about rounding up cows and killing them."

No one said a word, so Harold went on. "As we went, on our army got bigger and bigger, and more and more cows died. Every skull of every cow we brought back here to make us stronger. It was a heady time."

Harold looked like an old man, thinking back to his party days.

"When did Count Bovine show up?"

"Oh, about four months into our little war. He and five of his most powerful vampires walked in here one night and killed every one of my men without so much as a fight."

"Bet you thought you had it shielded, didn't you?" Aahz said.

"I did," Harold said. "I was so confident of the shielding that I didn't even have guards posted."

"Wouldn't have done any good," Aahz said. Tanda nodded. I didn't have a clue why he said that, but Harold seemed to agree as well.

"Needless to say, Count Bovine was angry. He imprisoned me up here, and put a spell on me so that every month, when he and his people are dining on my people, I'm a cow eating grass."

"How long ago was that?" I asked.

"I don't know exactly," Harold said. "No real reason to keep track. At least thirty years, maybe more."

"And Bovine and his people have been killing your people ever since?" Aahz asked, looking puzzled.

"Actually, no," Harold said. "That just started a few years back, when Count Bovine was killed and his second-in-command, Ubald, took over."

"Ubald's not one for keeping things in balance, is he?" Tanda asked.

"Not worried about it at all," Harold said. "He told me that there were enough of my kind around for his people to party for centuries."

"At least he didn't undo the cow spell," I said.

"Neither he nor Count Bovine could," Harold said. "Ubald keeps trying, though. He's using the cow skulls in the other room there to funnel energy into breaking it."

"Makes sense," Aahz said. "A spell that major, in place for that long, would be *almost* impossible to remove. But not *completely* impossible."

"He's got time," Harold said.

"So how did the map come about?" I asked.

"When Count Bovine was still alive, and had me locked up here, none of them lived anywhere near here. One day, this cartographer showed up. I wanted him to help me escape and he said he couldn't."

"He can't," Tanda said.

"Why?" I asked.

"He told me that, as long as he didn't involve himself in any activity in any dimension," Harold said, "he was free to use his magik to move anywhere he wanted, map anything he wanted, including through the magik that Count Bovine had put up to hold me here in this castle."

"I'm puzzled," Aahz said, "How did you get him to lie that there was a cow here who gave gold milk and draw a treasure map to it?"

"It never says anything about a cow giving gold milk," Harold said, laughing. "I'm the cow the map leads to, and I was willing to give anyone a lot of gold if they found me."

"Makes sense to me," Tanda said, laughing.

I was enjoying the different emotions playing over my mentor's face. We had deciphered the map, found the cow, and were entitled to the gold. That made Aahz's mouth water, I could tell. But, at the same time, getting the gold out of here, with all our blood still inside our bodies, was going to be another matter.

Harold noticed Aahz's face. "You're a Pervert, right?"

"Per*vect*," Aahz said, showing all his teeth.

He hated being called a Pervert, and often was, since that was the reputation of the demons from his dimension.

"Sorry," Harold said. "But you love money and gold, don't you?"

Now it was Tanda's and my turn to laugh. Aahz just gave us both a dirty look and then said, "Of course."

"You are welcome to all the treasure—gold if you want— you can carry from here," Harold said. "There's tons of the stuff in the back. The rocks of this mountain are full of it. All you have to do is help me escape."

I knew there wasn't a sunbeam's chance on Vortex #6 that Aahz would turn down that offer. But I didn't really mind. I sort of liked Harold. And besides, I'd lost a mentor once myself, and we apprentices needed to stick together.

"You know of a way to escape from here?" Tanda asked Harold, staring at how Aahz's eyes had glazed over at just the idea of a lot of gold.

"If I did, would I still be here?" he said, his voice sad.

Aahz looked at me and I shrugged. "Why not?"

Aahz looked at Tanda. Tanda sighed. "Sure. As you've been saying all along, we've come this far."

"Great," Aahz said. "We'll help you."

I knew for a fact that Aahz didn't have a clue how we were going to help Harold escape, but the promise sure cheered up our host.

After another hour of talking with Harold to make sure we hadn't missed anything important, I knew enough about this Ubald vampire guy to make me want another shot of carrot juice. The guy was just plain mean, almost as old as Count Bovine had been, and not at all happy with the situation as it stood.

On top of that, he liked to party, and party hard. By the time the sun was ready to come up on the last morning of the full moon, Harold said, Ubald and his group were stumbling idiots. Still very dangerous, but stumbling, and it often took the men with the golden shovels days to round up all the cattle from the different rooms of the castle and take them back to their private pastures.

The idea of coming into a huge bedroom suite to find two cows standing on a rumpled bed was too much for me. Tonight was that night, the most dangerous night of the full moon according to Harold. I could hardly wait.

Finally Aahz decided we had talked enough and we all headed back into the library area. Aahz wanted to have Harold show us the books about the spells put over this castle, the spells put on everyone by Count Bovine, and what Harold knew of the magik energy surrounding this castle.

But first we had to wake up Glenda. Snoring, drooling Glenda. As far as I was concerned, she could just stay right there, sleeping for the next hundred years, or until she died of hunger in her sleep, whichever came first.

But it seemed that Harold and Aahz had other ideas for her which they were not sharing with me.

"Are you confident she's cured?" I asked Harold as we stood staring at her.

"Completely," Harold said. "The magik rope there does the trick."

"Well, just to be sure," I said, "can we put the rope around her again tonight, before the sun sets?"

Aahz laughed. "Trust me, she'll have the rope on tonight. You can count on it."

I stared at him as he moved to her and untied the knot in the golden rope, then pulled it free, wrapping it in his hand.

After what Glenda had done to us, I figured it would have served her right to become a cow for most of every month for the rest of her life. She was already a self-centered bloodsucker; why shouldn't she have the entire cow package?

After Aahz pulled the rope off of her, she awoke, groaned and somehow managed to sit up, her face pale and her eyes glazed. "What happened?"

"You slept through the night just fine," Aahz said.

"Snoring like a horse," Tanda said.

I wanted to ask her how she knew horses snored, but figured this wasn't the time to push too much into her personal life.

Glenda's hand went to her neck, where there was now no sign of the vampire bites. I could tell that she was surprised when she touched her neck and it didn't hurt. Surprised and confused. Then she noticed the gold laced rope Aahz was holding. For a moment she looked into his eyes. Then she asked, "Was I going to turn?"

"You were," Harold said. "It was why Ubald and his vampire friends let you live."

"And the rope is what I think it is?" Glenda asked, not taking her eyes from Aahz.

Aahz held it up. "Just to be safe, you're going to wear it tonight as well. I promised my apprentice there for his peace of mind."

She stared at the rope for a moment, then nodded. "I suppose I should thank you."

"Just help us all get out of here and we can call it even," Aahz said.

"I'll do what I can," she said, "but first, can I have a glass of water?"

Harold laughed. "You *are* cured. I'll get it for you."

I had no idea why Harold thought that Glenda getting a glass of water meant she was cured. Seemed like a somewhat silly sign to me. Or maybe vampires were only thirsty for blood?

Harold headed out the panel toward his kitchen area. When he was safely gone Glenda looked up at Aahz, the anger clear and at full force in her eyes.

"Why didn't you just stake me when you had the chance?"

I was stunned by the question. And her anger at Aahz for not killing her.

"I thought about it," Aahz said.

He pointed to a sharp stake on top of an antique dresser beside the couch she was sitting on. I hadn't noticed it before. Again I was stunned. Aahz went on.

"I figure you can be of help to all of us, something you haven't done much of up to now."

"You know I'm going to have to wear that rope for the rest of my life," she said, "on every full moon, every time I hop dimensions, every night?"

"I know," Aahz said, his voice cold and low and sounding just about as mean as I had ever heard him sound. "And if you don't help us, I'm going to free you into the countryside here, in this dimension, without the rope. You'll be a cow for most of the rest of your life."

I stared at him, seeing a side of my mentor I didn't often see. It seemed that, as always, he had known more than he was telling me, and that helping her had just been a ruse to keep her with us and under his control. He tucked the rope into his pouch and crossed his arms.

"And if you want the rope to stay alive tonight, you're going to work with us and not pull any of your tricks. Understand?"

Glenda glared at him, then slowly nodded. "I understand."

Well, I didn't, but I didn't want anyone trying to explain it to me with all the anger flowing around at the moment.

Chapter Fifteen

"Go with the flow."
M. TWAIN

Sometimes in grand adventures, there are times when just nothing happens. The rest of the third day of the full-moon cycle was one of those times.

Aahz, Tanda, Harold, and Glenda spent the entire day poring over books and old scrolls, trying to find answers on how to get out. I mostly sat and listened, falling asleep every few minutes until my head bobbed enough to wake me up enough to listen until I fell asleep again.

And over and over that pattern went. My neck was sore by the time the day was over.

About thirty minutes before the sun set Aahz had Glenda lie down on a couch, and then he tied the gold-laced magikal rope around her. She fell asleep instantly. That rope was the best sleep aid I had ever seen. Aahz should take it back with us to Posseltum to make money. On bad nights, I bet the king would pay a ransom for it.

If it had been up to me, I'd have sent Glenda out into the hallway to be a cow, eating grass and being followed around by a guy in a white hat with a shovel. But it wasn't up to me, so Aahz put her to sleep.

About twenty minutes before the sun set Harold shut us into the library again and went to his grass to become a cow for the night.

I slept off and on all night. Aahz and Tanda did as well, reading while they were awake. By morning, when Harold opened the door and let in a few wonderful rays of sunlight from the living area, I was well-rested and bored to tears.

Aahz untied Glenda to wake her up, pouched the rope, and we all went out into the kitchen area to have Harold cook us horse steaks covered in tomatoes. He called it his celebration breakfast. He said he had it every month after the last full moon night.

I had to admit, it was surprisingly good.

After breakfast the talk turned to escape, which, after the boring day and the fear of cow vampires all night, was the most interesting topic I could imagine.

Aahz took charge of the discussion and ticked off our options. "First chance we have is to lower the dimension-hopping screen. If we could do that for even an instant, we'd be out of here."

"I've never run into a screen like it," Tanda said, "even in all my years of being an assassin. It's more solid than a rock."

"More than likely coming from the energy in the mountain," Aahz said.

I thought about the map on the ceiling, and how Aahz hadn't mentioned it to either Harold or Glenda. I had no idea what he was thinking, but I sure didn't want to mess up what he was doing by blurting something out. I'd done enough of that in the past.

"Our second option is to just find a way out of the castle."

"Right," I said, "and sneak all the way through Donner and past the posse."

"Posse?" Harold asked.

"Mounted riders who knew we were coming far outside of town."

"They picked me up as well," Glenda said.

"So they have some magik that tells them enemies are coming," Aahz said. "We could be screened against that."

"If we knew what kind of magik it was," Tanda said.

"I'm stuck here anyway," Harold said. He pointed to what I had assumed was the front door to the suite. "It's like walking into a wall trying to go through there."

"And the same for how we came in?" Tanda asked.

"Oh, I can go all the way to the entrance into the ballroom through the skull room," Harold said. "Then I hit the screen."

"How about through the floor, or the window?" I asked.

"Haven't tried either," he said.

"I doubt it would work," Aahz said.

"Yeah," Tanda said, "captive spells, which I think this sounds like, are all-around prisons. It's like being in an invisible, unbreakable bubble."

"So to get Harold out with us," I said, "we have to break that spell as well."

"You're coming with us?" Glenda asked.

"I'm going to try," Harold said. He didn't add that there was gold for getting him out, and none of the rest of us filled her in either.

"So, old mentor," I said to Aahz, "how do we go about breaking the spells, since it seems to me that both our main ways of escape are blocked by them?"

He looked at me with a harsh look, then answered my question. "A couple of ways to break a spell. Either put a counter-spell on it, or cut off the source of power to the spell."

"Since this place is flowing with energy, the second doesn't sound likely. How does a counter-spell work?"

"I've tried every one I know," Harold said.

I glanced at Aahz. "My mentor hasn't even taught me any yet."

"When you gain enough self-control to use them," Aahz said, "I might think about it."

"I tried a number of them the first day I was here," Glenda said. "Didn't even dent the dimension-hopping shield."

"I tried all the ones I knew as well," Tanda said, frowning. Since we were all still here, I assumed she had had the same result as Glenda.

"And I saw nothing in any of the books back there to give us any help either," Aahz said. "In fact, I think it's worse than we are assuming. I think the spell that keeps all the vampires as cows, and your people under their spell and not killing the cows every month, is tied up with the very spells we are trying to break."

"If that's the case," Harold said, sounding defeated, "to free me, I must release all my people from the spell that has held them for centuries, and free all the vampires to kill them at the same time. I can't do that."

"Actually," Aahz said, smiling, "there might be a way that it would work, if we could shut everything down at once and at an exact time."

"How?" Harold asked.

"I wouldn't mind knowing the same thing," I said.

Tanda laughed with Aahz. "Do it during the middle of the day."

I frowned and looked at Aahz, who was nodding and laughing at me. Harold was frowning as well.

Glenda was laughing, but not very much.

"All the cows are out in pastures," Aahz said, his voice taking on the tone he got when I was being so stupid he couldn't believe I could be that stupid.

"Daylight," Tanda said. "Vampires?"

"Oh," Harold said. "Of course. Sunlight kills vampires."

"Of course," I said out loud, pretending I had just forgotten, even though I had never known that fact about vampires. Why would I have? Until I came to this stupid dimension, I had never seen or even heard of a vampire. I just figured they had something to do with full moons.

"So if we shut off the power to the big spell somehow," Harold said, "all the vampires on one half of the planet would die."

"Exactly," Aahz said, "And the ones on the night side would have to find shelter by sunrise, giving your people time to kill many of them."

"Aahz, I just have one question."

He looked at me and said nothing.

"How do you propose to shut off the energy flowing in this area?"

Aahz smiled. "That's our problem, isn't it?"

"Why do I think I'm not going to like what you're thinking at this moment?"

"Oh, maybe because I'm thinking that's where *you're* going to come in."

Tanda laughed.

"It's not funny," I said.

"Sure it is," Tanda said.

I just stared at Aahz. Someday I'd love to figure out a way to get him his powers back so I wasn't the one doing the dirty work all the time. I had a hunch, from the look on his face, that this was going to get *really* dirty for me. Center-of-the-mountain-kill-the-energy-at-its-source dirty.

"Before we can figure out how to block the energy for the spells," Aahz said, "we have to know how it flows through the castle."

He said that and I just shuddered.

I could feel how much of the energy flowed in this place any time I opened my mind to it. It came from down in the mountain, flowing up and out. Usually energy for magik was in lines flowing through the sky that I had to reach up and tap to work a disguise spell, or a flying spell. Or, if there was no air energy, I went for ground energy flowing deep under the surface and rocks. Air energy was easier to get, and Aahz had taught me to always go for it first.

But this castle was built right on a place where energy flowed up from below and out into the sky in all directions. Mapping meant someone who could read energy lines had to somehow get above the castle and look down at it all.

"So what do we do?" Tanda asked. "How do we start doing that?"

"First," Aahz said, "we try to figure out how the energy flows into that skull room. It was strong and getting stronger in there right before all the cows turned to vampires the other night."

"Really?" Harold asked.

I was surprised that Aahz had wanted to start there, but it made sense. We had to map the energy patterns, and starting where we knew a lot was being tapped seemed logical.

Suddenly I realized what I had been thinking about.

"Map," I said aloud.

Everyone sort of turned and stared at me.

"Map," I said again, smiling at them. I reached into my pouch and pulled out the magik map we had used so often to get into this fix. If it got us here, it just might be able to get us out.

"Oh, heavens, yes," Aahz said, smiling at me. "Great thinking, Skeeve."

That was the third time he had complimented me on something to do with the map. I was going to have to keep this parchment with me at all times. Aahz hadn't given me that many compliments in the last year.

I opened up the map. It was completely blank. Nothing on it at all. For some reason, that wasn't what I was expecting. I'm not sure exactly what I *was* expecting, but a blank parchment just flat wasn't it.

"Perfect," Aahz said, looking at the empty sheet.

I handed it to him, flashing it so the others could tell it was blank as well. If he liked a map with no lines, he could have a map with no lines.

"Was that the map the cartographer did?" Harold asked. "The one that got you here?"

"Sure was," I said.

"What happened to it?" Harold asked.

"It got us here," Tanda said.

"Oh," Harold said.

"Tanda," Aahz said, "do you know how to do a mapping spell?"

Tananda shook her head. "Beyond me, I'm afraid."

"Glenda?"

"Nope," she said. "When I needed a map I went to a cartographer's booth on Deva and bought one."

"Same with me," Harold said.

Aahz turned and looked at me. "Guess it's up to you, apprentice."

"Okay," I said, "but don't you think I need a little practice at this spell first?"

Aahz held up the paper. "This is the only piece of magik paper we have. You only get one shot at it."

"No pressure," I said.

"If I didn't believe you could do it," Aahz said, "would I be wanting you to try?"

I didn't think I should remind him he had offered the job to everyone but me to start with. No point in ruining the mood when he was trying to boost my confidence. He did that less often than he complimented me.

"We'll be back shortly," Aahz said to everyone as he motioned for me to follow him, "I hope with a map."

"Yeah, me too," I said.

Aahz headed us across the carpet of grass. We had to sidestep around a pile of cow droppings on the way. I guess that Harold didn't have a man with a golden shovel standing behind him at night. At the hidden entrance to the skull room Aahz stopped and turned back to Tanda.

"Are we going to be shielded out there?"

"Doing magik?" Tanda asked. "Some, but it might show through."

I didn't like the sound of that. The last thing we needed up here was the posse.

Aahz stopped and thought for a minute. "How about in the back library area?"

"That's so shielded, nothing could get out," Tanda said.

"I agree," Harold said. "It would be much safer to do spells back there."

Aahz indicated I should follow him and again we went around the pile of cow droppings, across the room and through the bathroom to the old library. I had spent so much time in this room already, I really didn't want to be in here again. Aahz pushed the door closed behind him, then laid the empty paper on top of the desk he had sat at last night.

"This is going to work even better in here," he said. "I want you to do this in two parts."

"Give it to me clearly and I'll try."

My mentor nodded. "First, we're going to imprint that ceiling map on this paper."

I glanced up, then back at Aahz. "Good idea. How do I do that?"

"This part is going to be pretty easy," Aahz said. "Simpler than flying or doing disguise spells."

I nodded. I liked the sound of simple at this point. Since I was only getting one try, simple was the best.

"Open your mind, take in the energy as you have practiced, controlling the flow to a medium level."

"Now?" I asked.

"Now," he said.

I did as he instructed. Since we had been together I had practiced this so much it had become almost second nature to me. I could do it almost instantly when needed. When we first left my old mentor's cabin, Aahz had told me that would happen, but back then it had been so hard to do I didn't believe him.

Now, reaching out with my mind and getting energy was easy, and with this much energy flowing around me, the trick was getting only enough so that I could control what I was doing.

"Got it," I said after a moment. The energy flow was moving through me, ready to power anything I told it to.

"Now, in one motion," Aahz said, "without a break, picture the map on the ceiling and then picture the same map on the paper."

I did it, letting the energy help me get a clear image of the ceiling map, then a clear image of the same lines and shapes and words on the magik paper.

I let go of the energy and opened my eyes.

"Perfect," Aahz said, actual excitement in his voice.

I glanced at the roof. The map was still there. Good, I hadn't harmed it.

Then I looked at the paper, almost afraid of what I might see. The same map was reproduced there, only the lines were much clearer, and there were words on the paper that I didn't remember even seeing on the ceiling. And none of the dust and dirt obscured it either. I couldn't believe it. I had done a new spell perfectly the first time!

"Now don't go getting a swollen head," Aahz said, as if he could read my thoughts. "That was the easy part."

I didn't care. I had done it, and done it right the first time. For the moment that was all that mattered.

"So what's next?"

"We do the same spell with energy lines," Aahz said, "imprinting them on this map of the castle."

I knew that was what he was going to want, but doing that meant stepping out of my mind to look down on the energy lines through the entire area. And the last time I had tried that I almost hadn't made it back inside my own mind. Of course, Aahz didn't know I had even tried. I didn't want to tell him because I knew he'd be angry.

"This is going to take some preparation," Aahz said.

"I'd hoped it would."

He put the map on the floor and had me stand right over it. "See the images there?"

I nodded, staring down at the map I had just created. It was a beautiful thing indeed. "Now, when we start," Aahz said, "I want you to imagine yourself floating above the energy lines, above the castle if you have to, in the same fashion you use to reach out for the energy lines in a spell."

"Okay," I said, still staring down at the map at my feet, "but isn't there a risk I will just float away?" Standing above the map like this, it almost felt as if I was already floating.

"Good question, apprentice," Aahz said. "Just put a string on your foot."

"A what?" I looked up into my mentor's eyes. I could tell he was concerned with me even trying this. I didn't know if the concern was for me, or for what would happen if I failed, but at least he was concerned.

"A string, like a kid's balloon string," he said. "Imagine one tied from the foot of your real body to the foot of your imaginary body as it floats upward. Then when you want to return, just go back down the string."

I nodded. That was such a simple image, even I might be able to handle it.

"When you get a good view of all the flowing energy lines over and through the castle," Aahz said, "just do what you did with this map. Imagine them as you see them; then' in one motion imagine them on the paper."

"Okay," I said. "I think I can do that."

"When you're ready," Aahz said, stepping back. "Just do it."

I looked at the map at my feet, putting the image clearly in my head. Then I let myself go.

That is what it actually felt like. I was letting go of what was holding me down. I was floating upward. I checked to make sure I had a string attached to my foot. It was there, so I relaxed and just kept going, floating upward.

I went above the energy line I had used to create the other map, through the roof of the castle, and then stopped, floating right over the top of the golden castle in the beautiful sunshine.

Below me rivers of blue energy flowed, coming up out of the middle of the castle like a well, splitting and flowing off in dozens of directions over the mountains and valleys.

I let my mind accept all the different levels of energy flow, all the way down into the deepest area of the castle. I could see all the streams, all the different places they branched, and all the places they were tapped.

Then, when I had them all, I held the image, imprinted it on my mind, and then imagined it being overlaid in blue lines on the map at my feet.

It only took an instant. Then, with one last look at the beautiful colors of the energy and the surrounding country-side, I tugged on the string attached to my foot and I was back in my body, just like that.

I opened my eyes and glanced at Aahz. My mentor was smiling like he had just won all the riches of the Bazaar at Deva.

"Amazing," he said. "Sometimes you just flat amaze me."

I was afraid to look down, so instead I stepped back.

Aahz picked up the map and held it for me to see. There, in black lines, was the first map of the castle I had done from the ceiling.

And over it were flowing lines of energy. The magik of the map was keeping the lines flowing in the image, just as I had seen it from above.

I didn't know what to say. He was holding something I had created, and it was beautiful and working as it should.

Better than it should. I had never expected the energy lines to keep moving, but they were.

"Come on, apprentice. Let's go show the rest what you did. Amazing, simply amazing."

He turned and headed for the door.

For the first time in all our time together, I had sensed a little pride in Aahz's voice. I might have been imagining it, but this time I didn't think so.

It was pride, and it made me feel good.

Chapter Sixteen

"Put your name on the map."
A. VESPUCCI

Everyone made great noises about the map I had created. And Tanda gave me a long and very nice hug. I didn't say much, since I was so proud of what I had done, I was afraid I'd ruin the moment by saying something stupid.

Finally, Aahz laid the map out on the table and said, "Let's get to work. We need to find on here where the spell Count Bovine placed over this dimension is drawing its power."

I studied the moving blue lines with everyone else, watching how they seemed to come up out of the floor plan of the castle and into the air.

The map was magik, so it even showed the different levels of the castle, like looking into a fishbowl. It was both beautiful and disconcerting at the same time.

"Look in the sub-level of the castle," Tanda said, pointing.

I let my eyes adjust so that I could see the plan of the castle that far down. I instantly saw what she was pointing at. The wide, thick river of energy that was pouring up from the ground suddenly thinned, like a good part of it had been drained away into an unseen drain. That unseen drain, using that much energy, could only be a spell large enough to control an entire dimension.

"I think you have it," Aahz said, nodding.

"I agree," I said, remembering what the energy below that point felt like while I had been floating, and what it felt like above that point.

"Where did you get this floor plan?" Harold asked, staring at it. "I've never seen anything like this before. That corridor isn't there, and I have no idea what that tunnel goes to."

I glanced at Aahz, who only smiled.

"You've seen this before," I said. "It's painted on the ceiling of the library in there."

"No, it's not," Harold said, shaking his head. "This is a picture of the castle during Count Bovine's first days."

"Go look for yourself," Tanda said. "It took me a while to see it as well. Skeeve spotted it first."

Harold stared at us as if we had all gone nuts. I didn't blame him. If I had been living in a place for as many years as he had been trapped here, and a stranger had pointed something this important out, I wouldn't believe him either.

He huffed and stormed off toward the library.

"Okay," I said, "we know where Count Bovine tapped into the energy stream. How do we untap it?"

"We have to get down there," Aahz said. "Then we have to divert it for just an instant to break the link. That's all it will take."

I looked at the massive flow of energy rushing up out of the ground. I could tap into small energy streams, but I had no idea how a person would go about blocking something this large. And I wasn't sure I wanted to ask.

Harold came back in, looking stunned and embarrassed.

"If we manage to block this," Tanda said, "what do you think will happen?"

Aahz looked at the map. "Probably every spell ever put up by any of Count Bovine's people will be broken."

"My people will have their minds and free will back," Harold said.

"Yeah," I said, "and every vampire will suddenly be around every day of every month."

"Half of the population of vampires will be dead moments after they turn from cows," Aahz said. "And all the others will be without resources, clothes, shelter, and food, with the sun coming quickly."

"Do you think my people will remember all the years of having to submit to the round-up?" Harold asked.

"I have no doubt," Aahz said. "You still remember it before you were rescued from here, don't you?"

Harold nodded. "My people will hunt down and kill most of the remaining vampires."

"And you'll be free to leave," I said.

"If we can break the vampire hold on my world, I won't want to leave," Harold said. "I'll stay here and help my people rebuild."

I shook my head. It was all fine and good to plan what people would do if we succeeded, but I sure didn't see that happening any time soon.

"So no one has answered the question yet of how we stop that flow."

I didn't even want to try to bring up the point of getting down to that spot in the castle. We were way up at the top, and that breach in the main flow was way down in a sub-basement, where I doubted anyone had been in centuries.

"Gold," Glenda said, her voice sounding tired and worn. "Gold would stop the flow, if you could focus enough of it."

Aahz seemed to be off somewhere inside his head, thinking. Tanda was doing the same thing.

Harold and I looked at each other. Clearly, as apprentice magicians, neither of us even had a clue what the other three were considering.

"I think it might be done," Aahz said, nodding. He looked at Glenda. "Good idea."

She said nothing in return. It seemed that as the closer we got to a possible answer, the more sullen and reserved she became. I was still so angry at her for what she did to me that I didn't care enough to even ask what was happening.

"Okay, to the next problem," I said. "How do we get down there with enough gold to stop the energy stream?"

"We won't need much gold," Tanda said. "Just enough, with a good connection spell, to hook other nearby gold into the blockage. Maybe something gold-plated and flat."

"A golden shovel?" I asked.

Tanda nodded. "That would do it, I'm sure."

Harold moved over toward the front door of the suite, near where the grass was planted. He tapped a spot on the wall and a closet door opened. He reached inside and pulled out a golden shovel, just like the ones the palace guys had. It seemed that, in the palace, no cow droppings could be picked up with anything but a golden shovel.

"Okay, we're set for the gold part," Aahz said. "Tanda, when we're ready to try this, can you do the connection spell to hook enough gold into the shovel?"

She nodded. "I've done a number of them over the years to build shields and walls."

"So back to my problem," I said. "How do we get down there without being run over by the mounted posse?"

Aahz pointed to a spot on the map. At first I couldn't see what he was pointing at, then I saw it. The very same tunnel I had been afraid I was going to end up down in.

"Follow where it leads," Aahz said. "Starting with the secret opening back in the library."

I did as he suggested, focusing on the map as it changed, showing me the different levels of the secret passageway as it dropped through the mountain behind the castle, curved under everything, and came out in the very room where the big energy flow had been taken off for the spell.

"Looks like there was a reason that tunnel was built," Aahz said, smiling at me.

"Count Bovine used it to get to his main power source when he lived here full-time," Harold said.

"What do you know?"

"So we're going underground," I said, reaching over and taking the heavy shovel from Harold. "I just hope I don't have to dig my way out."

"You and me both," Aahz said, staring at the map.

My mentor had a way of making everything seem so positive that it was a wonder I could even move most mornings.

It took a little longer than I had expected to find the hidden passageway into the tunnel in the old library. We had to move pile of furniture, old books, and more rolled-up scrolls than I could count. The scrolls were the hardest, since Harold wouldn't let us just kick them aside. Finally, we got to the spot where the passage should be and faced a stone wall.

"I didn't think there was anything back here," he said. "After all these years, I know this room."

I didn't want to mention to him that he really didn't, since he hadn't even noticed the map painted on the ceiling.

"Oh, it's here all right," Aahz said.

All five of us were standing there in the dusty place. I had the shovel, Tanda had the map.

"Glenda?" Aahz said.

She stepped up to him.

Quicker than I had seen my mentor move in a long, long time, Aahz had the rope out of his pouch, over her head, and tied.

She dropped to the ground, sound asleep, before she could even get a complaint out of her mouth. I was stunned.

"Harold," Aahz said, "pick up her feet and let's move her to a couch."

Harold looked as stunned as I felt. Tanda seemed to again know exactly what was happening. Aahz moved Glenda to the couch, made sure the rope was tied, then looked at Harold. "No matter what you do, what you think, what happens around you, do not untie her until we get back. Understand?"

Harold nodded. "But I don't see why."

"The map," Aahz said.

Tanda held it up and pointed to a spot on it.

"Right here," she said. "See this tiny thin line coming up out of the basement and into this suite?"

I looked real close. For a moment I thought she was making it up, then I saw the blue line. It went right to a spot in the suite where the chair was, where Glenda had been sitting when I did the map.

"Glenda's hooked up somehow," Aahz said. "I didn't see that until we had already made our plans."

"You mean they might know we're coming?"

"Possible," Aahz said.

"Oh, that's nice," I said. I wondered how many of that posse I could hit with the golden shovel before they took it away from me.

"Are you ready?" Aahz asked.

"You want me to lead?" I asked, still not seeing where we were going to go.

"I've got it for the moment," Aahz said. He picked up the torch we had brought with us from the first tunnel, held it out and said to me, "A light might help."

I eased some energy out of the stream, just enough to start the torch on fire. Not long ago I had had trouble with that spell as well. And a year ago I might have set the entire library on fire trying to light that torch.

"Follow me," Aahz said, and stepped at the stone wall.

And right through it.

"This place could give a guy a headache," I said, moving at the stone wall behind him. I had the shovel slightly in front of me in case the stone decided to be stone for me.

I went right through, just as Aahz had done.

Tanda came through behind me.

The tunnel was narrow and carved out of solid rock. Steps led down into the bowels of the earth. More steps than I could see in the torchlight. The place was cold and very dusty. It was clear that no one had been in here in a very, very long time, as our footsteps kicked up a cloud of dust that swirled in the flickering light of the torch.

"Are we shielded?" Aahz asked Tanda.

"Same as in the library," Tanda said. "Count Bovine didn't want this tunnel found, that's for sure."

"That helps us," I said.

Aahz nodded, made sure we were both ready, then, holding the torch up so that we could see the steps as well as he could in the dust, he started down.

And we went down for a very, very long time, kicking up thick clouds of dust with every step. I could not imagine how anyone could have carved the tunnel. I could barely walk the steps, and we were going down. Climbing this must be next to impossible for anyone not in top shape.

Finally, after what seemed like a nightmarish eternity, we reached an area of the tunnel that flattened out.

"Map," Aahz said.

Tanda moved up and the two of us crowded with Aahz so that we could see the map in the torchlight and swirling dust. It showed that we had reached the bottom of the tunnel. I glanced around at the rock walls and ceiling. We were under thousands and thousands of body-lengths of rock. I couldn't imagine how much weight was pressing down on the ceiling of the tunnel above us right at that moment.

The thought sent a shiver through me, and a touch of panic.

"Can we keep going?" I asked.

Tanda took the map and Aahz smiled at me, his green scales covered in dust, his eyes yellow holes in the dirt. I must have looked as bad as he did, maybe worse.

"A little claustrophobia?" he asked.

"I don't know about that," I said, not having a clue what the big word meant. Sometimes Aahz just didn't remember what a backward part of a backward world I came from.

"Feeling the pressure of all this weight over us?" Tanda asked.

"Yeah," I said, "more than I want to think about right now, thank you very much."

Aahz laughed. "We don't have that much farther to go."

"Then let's go," I said, fighting against the panic at the walls closing in.

Aahz gave me a long look, then turned and headed along the flat part of the tunnel. I kept the golden shovel clutched in front of me. At least if the tunnel came down, I'd be buried with something worth digging up. After a hundred paces the tunnel started back up. Stair after stair after stair. Up and up and up.

I forgot to be afraid of the tunnel coming down on me because I was so tired from the climbing.

"Wait," Aahz said, stopping to pant for a moment. "The air's bad in here."

I realized when he said that that I was also having trouble getting enough air. Now not only was the roof about to fall and crush me, I was going to die from lack of air.

"Almost there," Tanda said from behind me. I could hear the rustling of the map. Aahz nodded and pushed upward, taking one step at a time.

I used the shovel as a sort of crutch. *Step. Clunk. Step. Clunk.*
The sound echoed down the tunnel behind us. If this plan
didn't work, I couldn't imagine having to go back to the suite
using this tunnel. I'd try it if I had to, but I sure didn't want to.
Step. Clunk. Step. Clunk.

We kept climbing. Forever. How could this be? Had we
gotten turned around and were headed back to the suite?

My lungs burned like the time I had stayed underwater too
long in the pond when I was a kid. My eyes stung with the
dust, and I could feel the grit in my mouth.

"We're here," Aahz said, his voice barely a whisper. I glanced
back. Tanda was a few steps behind me, her face covered in
dust, mud caked around her mouth and nose. She looked as if
she was about to pass out.

Ahead of me Aahz slid back a wooden panel and stepped
through.

Cool, fresh air hit me like a hammer as I stepped up to
follow him. In all my life I couldn't remember anything feeling that good before.

We were in a good-sized room, at least fifty paces across,
that was completely empty of every stick of furniture. It was
simply four walls of stone, a stone floor, and a stone ceiling.
From the looks of it, the door we had come through was the
only door in the place. And there were no windows. Where
the wonderful fresh air was coming from I had no idea.

"Oh, my," Tanda said, coming up out of the tunnel and
taking big gulping breaths of air. I gulped right along with her.

Aahz came over and took the map from Tanda, studying it
as we caught our breath. After a moment he moved around
the room, staying to the outside.

I knew why he stayed to the outside. In the center of the
room was a massive energy flow coming up through the floor
and going out through the ceiling. It wouldn't hurt him to
walk through it, but Aahz was taking no chances.

About halfway around the room he stopped, studied the
map again, and then came back toward us a few steps.

"Right here," he said, pointing into the empty air. "Right
here is where the energy flow is diverted."

He pointed in the direction of the empty wall beside him, indicating how the energy flow moved off the main one.

I took a deep breath and let my mind open slightly to see the flow.

"Wow!" I said, staggering backwards from the sight.

Beside me Tanda did the same.

"It's huge!" she said.

Not more than a few paces in front of me was a torrent of pure blue energy, flowing like a fast-moving river up out of the ground and through the ceiling. It was a good forty or more paces across. I could see Aahz through it, but just barely. About halfway up, in the center of the room about head high, the flow seemed to decrease in size significantly, from forty paces across to less than thirty. I could see where the other energy was going sideways and then vanishing in the direction that Aahz had pointed. That energy was powering the spell that held this dimension in the strange state it was in. How Count Bovine had managed to divert so much energy into one spell was also beyond my apprentice's level of understanding. I glanced down at the little gold shovel I held in my hand, then back at the raging torrent of blue energy in front of me. The silliness of even thinking of trying to change that torrent with my little shovel made me laugh.

Aahz, staying to the outside, came back around to where we were standing.

"This isn't possible," I said, holding up the shovel.

"It fills this room, Aahz," Tanda said, the awe in her voice clear. "I've never seen an energy stream anything like it."

"We can do it," Aahz said. Again I looked at my little gold shovel, then at the torrent of blue energy and just shook my head. Sometimes my mentor was smart, sometimes angry, but right now he was just plain crazy.

Chapter Seventeen

"I've heard of goldbricking, but this is ridiculous"
MIDAS REX

"Skeeve," Aahz said, "can you see where the flow for Count Bovine's spell leaves the main energy?"

We had moved around to the side of the room where Count Bovine's spell took its energy from the river of flowing energy pouring out of the ground.

"Yes, right in front of us," I said.

I pointed out where it left and how high it was to Aahz, who nodded.

I was using a part of my mind that allowed me to reach out for energy and do spells myself. That part allowed me to see the energy, where Aahz, who had lost his powers, could not.

Where the energy for Count Bovine's spell left the main stream was like a branch on a big tree. It sort of cut it off of one side of the main flow, moving up and sideways. The moment the secondary flow was sideways to the main one, it vanished into the spell it was being used for. We had about a body length, right above where I stood, to cut that side-flow off and send it along in the main flow. At least, that was the theory on what we were going to try. Sort of like trying to dam up the side branch of a river in one quick move, without getting wet. But even that side-branch of this energy, where I could see it, had to be ten paces across. Far, far wider than my little gold shovel. Yet from what I understood, Aahz wanted me to try to divert or even stop that energy with my shovel. Not a chance in a Bovine hell.

Aahz moved over behind me. "We're going to have to do this together," he said. "Tanda, when I say 'ready' you connect the gold in this shovel to whatever gold you can sense nearby. Pull in as much as you can."

"Oh, so you're going to make the shovel bigger?" I asked, starting to understand his plan.

"Exactly," he said.

Tanda nodded. "I'm going to have to make the gold wide, at least ten feet around."

Tanda could see the giant flow of energy as well as I could. She also knew how insane this attempt was.

"I know," Aahz said, nodding.

"Can you hold that much?" I asked. "I sure can't."

"We're both going to try," Aahz said. "You steer, I'll lift. I'm going to get under the shovel. When Tanda connects other gold to it and starts expanding it, it's going to get really, really heavy very quickly, so be ready the moment I say go. I don't want to drop it."

I nodded. This gold-plated shovel wasn't that light as it was. I couldn't imagine how Aahz and I could even try to hold up a gold block ten feet across, even a thin one.

"We have to keep it out of the flow until it's big enough," Aahz said.

"Okay," I said. "Let's do this and get on to the next life."

Aahz laughed. "That's what I like about you, apprentice. Always a good mental attitude."

"Give me something to be positive about," I said.

Aahz moved around and got under me, bracing himself solidly as I held the shovel up in position next to the side-flow of energy. When the gold got big enough for what Tanda was going to do, we were going to simply let the shovel fall to our right and cut off the side-flow to the spell. However, if we let the shovel fall forward into the main flow, there was no telling what would happen.

Aahz said he wasn't even sure what was going to happen when we cut the side-flow. He hoped nothing, but he didn't know for sure when I had asked him.

"Ready!" Aahz shouted, even though the room was empty and there were only the three of us in it.

To an outsider watching us who couldn't see the energy flow, we would have looked darned silly. Aahz crouched in front of me, holding onto the shovel I was holding in the air. Tanda beside us, her head tilted back, staring up into nothingness.

"Ready," she said.

I knew she was sending her mind out, linking gold, pulling it in to add to our shield.

"Now!" Aahz shouted again.

Instantly the shovel started growing in size and in weight. I braced myself as Aahz did the same. I was stunned at how heavy it got so quickly.

The shovel grew and I strained against dropping it, trying to do my job of just holding it steady.

"About half!" Aahz said, his voice strained from holding up the ever-heavier shovel. Aahz was one of the strongest demons I knew, and he was having problems. I did my best to help lift at the same time as holding the shovel in position. I doubted I was doing much good, but I knew for a fact the effort was going to cost me later.

The shovel was getting bigger and bigger, growing quicker and quicker.

"Almost!" Aahz said, his voice barely a croak under the weight. Above me the shovel looked like a massive gold coin.

"Now!" Aahz said.

I pushed sideways, letting the shovel fall toward the side-flow of energy as Tanda kept adding more and more gold to it.

Like a gold knife, the shovel cut through the blue energy.

At that moment everything in the room seemed to explode.

I was smashed back against the stone, banging my head hard.

Tanda tumbled across the floor toward the door, coming to rest pressed against the wood. Her eyes were closed and I couldn't tell if she was hurt or not.

Aahz was pressed against the stone wall beside me.

Forces like I had never felt before held me in position as the gold cut through the flow just as we had planned. So far it was working. I couldn't believe it.

But then the shovel kept growing and growing as more and more gold poured into it. Something was wrong. Tanda should have unlinked the gold in the shield we built from the other gold around the area when the shield hit the energy. But there was clearly still more and more gold pouring into that shield. It had cut the side-flow, but now it was falling slowly toward the main flow, cutting into it as well as it kept growing.

Then the room seemed to expand outward and the pressure of my head against the stone sent me down into a blackness I didn't much like.

"Skeeve!"

"Skeeve! Can you hear me?"

The voice sounded far off, like it was coming from over a hill. I didn't care. It was still dark out and I wanted to sleep some more.

"Skeeve!"

The voice was getting closer, or so it seemed. I was in blackness. Pitch-black blackness. I tried to open my eyes, but everything still remained black. Every muscle in my body ached, and somehow I seemed to have fallen out of bed.

"Skeeve, if you can hear me, light the torch."

Now I understood the blackness, but I still couldn't remember where I was. I could hear something moving around, but it was so dark, I couldn't see a thing. More than likely it was Aahz trying to figure out what had happened to the lights.

I felt around on the floor beside me, but I couldn't find a torch. There wasn't one near me. I'm not sure why I expected there to be on the floor, but still I couldn't find it. The floor I was on was cold, like stone, and hard as a rock.

"Skeeve, some light."

Aahz was starting to get on my nerves. It was dark out. Why couldn't he just let me sleep? I reached down and ripped off a little piece of my shirt. I seemed to remember that some time in the past I had done that same thing. But the memory was foggy.

Holding the piece of cloth up in front of me, I focused my mind, trying to find some energy to take and light the cloth. It was hard, but I finally found enough to catch the cloth and start a small flame.

The room around me flickered into being. Aahz was sitting against a stone wall with Tanda's head on his lap about ten paces from me. There was nothing else in the room except a big hunk of thin, gray metal covering the center of the room.

"I was worried about you, apprentice," Aahz said. "Glad to see you alive."

"I was worried about me as well," I said.

Slowly I was remembering. We were here to cut the energy from a big spell done a long time ago by a Count Bovine, and the big pancake-like gray thing in the middle of the floor was my shovel, or what was left of it.

Tanda moaned on Aahz's lap and tried to sit up.

"Take it easy," Aahz said. "You got a nasty bump on the head."

"I can feel that," Tanda said. Then she looked around and smiled at me. "Good to see you made it as well."

"I'll tell you in the morning if I made it ," I said as more memories flooded back in.

She laughed and then clutched her head from the pain.

"I told you to go slow," Aahz said.

"Well," Tanda said after a moment. "Did we succeed?"

"I don't know," Aahz said. "Skeeve, did we succeed?"

It took me a moment of sitting there with my back against the wall and the cloth burning in my hand to understand what he wanted me to do. Then it dawned on me. Look to see if the energy flow to the Bovine spell had stopped.

I could do that. Or at least I thought I could do that. I opened up my mind, searching for the blue energy stream that had filled this room just a short time ago. Nothing. The side stream and the main stream were now gone completely. The room was as empty energy-wise as it was furniture-wise.

"Oh, yeah," I said. "We succeeded. Maybe a little too well."

"All gone?" Tanda asked, not moving her head.

"All gone, main stream and all."

"Well, that's going to be interesting," Aahz said.

The cloth was starting to get close to burning my fingers, so I scooted slowly over on the floor to where the torch lay and lit it. Then I held it up and looked around. On the other side of the room, where I was fairly sure there hadn't been a door before, was now an open archway. A breeze blew in from the archway, through the room, and into the tunnel we had come out of.

"I think we'd better go see what we've done," Aahz said. "Can you both walk?"

I tested my legs as Tanda tested hers. It seemed that, besides a lot of bumps and bruises, we had all come out of everything pretty well. It was going to be interesting to see how the rest of the inhabitants of this castle fared.

"Do we have to go back up the tunnel?" I asked, trying to imagine making that climb in the condition I was in.

Aahz shook his head. "If this didn't work to stop Bovine's spell, nothing is going to, and that means we're never getting out of here, so why bother continuing to hide?"

"I thought *I* had the positive attitude," I said.

"I can learn from an apprentice," Aahz said.

We limped our way toward the door with the wonderful fresh breeze blowing in. It led us into a corridor that turned after about fifty paces. After the turn there was a flight of stairs. Painful stairs, but at least stairs that had fresh air blowing down them.

At the top, the corridor turned again and went out an archway covered in a mass of flowering plants. Aahz pushed through the plants and I helped Tanda follow.

We stepped out into the beautiful sunshine of a wonderful afternoon. After being under tons of rock, getting knocked out by an energy explosion, and waking up in pitch darkness, the sunshine was beyond words.

There was a shovel lying on the lawn in front of us. It was the same shape as the golden-plated shovel we had used, only there was no gold left on it.

"Would you look at that," Aahz said.

On the corner of the lawn was a smoking pile of what looked like a cow.

"Looks like we broke Bovine's spell," I said.

"Sure does," Tanda said, pointing to the shovel. "On both sides of it. Whoever had that shovel has left. And the front gates of the castle are standing wide open."

She was right, but what I also noticed was that the gold trim that had decorated the gate was gone, and the gold along the top of the walls was gone. I looked slowly around. There wasn't a speck of gold in sight. Tanda's spell must have used it all around this area.

We walked across the soft grass toward the burning pile until the smell stopped us twenty feet away. It had been a vampire cow all right, but now its legs were sticking straight up in the air and its skin was burnt to a crisp. It looked as if had burst into flames and died almost instantly, before even turning completely back into its vampire form.

"What a waste," Aahz said, staring at the burning creature.

"What are you talking about?" I asked. "That was a blood-sucking vampire."

"No," Aahz said, shaking head. "I mean what a waste of good meat. No one eats their steak well-done these days."

He turned and smiled at me. "What was the chef thinking?"

"That it will be years before I eat another steak," I said.

Chapter Eighteen

"So where's the profit?"
TERECTUS

Victorious or not, we were still pretty tired by the time we made our way back to where we had left Harold and Glenda. Something I've noticed in the past about playing with channeling energies: when it's over, what you feel is drained.

The first thing that was noticeable was that apparently Harold had untied Glenda, as she was conscious and perched in a chair across the table from him. The second was that Harold himself seemed far more composed as he rose to greet us.

"Ah, my friends! It seems that congratulations are in order," he said, smiling broadly. "All indications are that you were successful in your efforts to shut down the spells."

"That's not all that's in order," Aahz said darkly, folding his arms across his chest. "I think, at this point, we're due a few explanations. Beyond the tale you told us originally, that is."

"But of course," Harold said, gesturing for us to pull up chairs. "I take it that you have already determined that my story was not quite complete."

"Let's just say that the facts as they were presented to us don't quite add up," Tananda said through tight lips.

Harold nodded. "It is true that there were a few minor points that I omitted or altered slightly when I explained the situation you."

"Why don't you just fill us I on those points now," Aahz said, "and let us decide for ourselves how minor they are."

"Very well. First, perhaps things will be clearer if I admit that my name is not Harold. In truth, I am Count Bovine himself."

"The vampire?" I said, not able to keep the horror and fear from my voice.

"I am the Count," said Harold/Bovine, "but a vampire no longer. That, perhaps, is at the heart of the dilemma I found myself in."

"You'll recall my telling you about my old mentor, Leila. Well, one of the things she taught me was how to shed the trappings and needs of a vampire and to lead a normal life. That is, as normal as life can be for one who practices magik."

I could identify with that last observation, but the Count was continuing.

"We returned to this dimension with the intent of converting my fellow vampires into regular humans, thus allowing all the inhabitants to live and work together as equals. Unfortunately, the other vampires did not share my humanitarian views and wished to continue their roles are masters and rulers. That was when I attempted to lead the humans in a uprising, which ended with my mentor's death and my being imprisoned here. It was Ubald who attacked us. Other than that, my story was essentially true."

"So why didn't you tell us this in the first place?" Tananda said. "We might have helped out for a worthy cause."

"Perhaps," said Bovine. "Unfortunately it has been my experience that it is easier to get people to assist you out of motives of greed than of good will. Particularly if you are a vampire, or a converted vampire, seeking aid from humans."

"Speaking of which," Aahz said, "I believe there was some mention of a reward?"

Bovine spread his hands expressively.

"What can I say?" he said. "When I made my offer I was quite sincere, but I hadn't anticipated that your solution to the cow spell was going to convert all the gold in the dimension to lead."

I glanced around the suite, and saw that what he said was apparently true. Where once there was gold in abundance in the decorations and trim, there was now nothing but a dull, silverish metal.

"What I *really* hoped," Bovine continued, "was that I could convince you to stick around for a while and help me re-establish order here. You've all obviously been around the dimensions, and your knowledge and experience would be invaluable. I'm sure that, in the long run, we could work something out to compensate you for your time."

"I think that's my cue to be moving on," Glenda said, rising to her feet. "World-building is definitely not my cup of tea. It's time for me to cut my losses and head for home."

"What? Without your share of the reward?" Tanda said tersely.

"Big deal," Glenda said. "An equal share of nothing is nothing."

"Don't you mean two equal shares?" I said quietly.

For several heartbeats the whole room looked at me with blank expressions. Then Glenda giggled.

"So, you finally figured it out, did you?"

"You're the Shifter from the Bazaar. Right?" I said. "You jumped ahead of us to try to cut yourself in for two shares instead of one, and even tried to ditch us so you could keep it all for yourself."

"Hey! You can't blame a girl for trying." Glenda shrugged. "After having seen so many parties come traipsing through trying to follow that map, I figured I'd try tagging along and see if I could make a difference. I mean, I had a lot of effort invested in this treasure hunt, but hadn't seen even a copper in return so far."

"But when you first met us on Vortex, you said you weren't a Shifter," Tanda said.

"I lied." Glenda said simply. "One of the most closely guarded secrets of Shifters is that we can hold one shape if we set our minds to it. When Skeeve here asked me so abruptly, I thought he was guessing, so I ran a little bluff. I'm a bit curious as to how he figured it out."

"At the time, I was guessing," I admitted. "I didn't really put it together until after you ditched me on Kowtow."

I looked over at Aahz and Tanda.

"I know you both thought I was making a fool of myself over a pretty face when I let Glenda sucker me so badly," I said, "and to a certain degree you were justified. I know me better than you do, though, and the more I thought about it I couldn't believe I had been that gullible. Then I remembered the compulsion spell from the Shifter hut. That was it, wasn't it, Glenda? It's my guess that I'm exceptionally sensitive to that particular spell, and the residuals were enough to guarantee my co-operation."

"Close enough," she said. "Actually, I had it on at a lower strength when I was working with you, and had it vectored so the others wouldn't feel it and guess what was going on. I didn't think you had enough experience to realize what was going on. My mistake."

"I'll say it is," Tanda said. "Nice work, Skeeve."

"Well, as I was saying, I guess it's time for me to take off."

"Not so fast," Aahz said. "First, are we all in agreement that your failure to deal with us in good faith negates any and all deals we have together?"

"Sure." Glenda shrugged. "Like I say, one or two or no shares of nothing is still nothing."

"Then, too," Aahz smiled, "I'm sure you wouldn't like to have it bandied about the Bazaar that you've been poaching on your clients expeditions, would you? That wouldn't do your reputation much good, or the reputation of Shifters in general."

Glenda's eyes narrowed dangerously.

"Are you threatening me?"

"Not at all." Aahz said, showing his teeth again. "In fact, you can count on our silence and discretion. We will not mention this adventure or your role in it ever again, even amongst ourselves."

"Really?"

"...For a price."

"I knew it." Glenda said, rolling her eyes. "Perverts!"

"That's Per-*vects*," I said, "and that little slip of the tongue is going to cost you extra."

Aahz positively beamed at me before turning his attention to Tanda.

"Tanda, dear?" he said. "How would you like to accompany Glenda here home and settle the details of our agreement while Skeeve and I finish up here? The Bazaar is a much better atmosphere for negotiating. We'll use the D-Hopper and catch up with you at Posseltum."

"Love to." Tanda smiled. "Come along, sweetheart. We have a long talk ahead of us."

The two ladies stood close, then disappeared with a soft BAMF. Glenda hadn't even bothered to say goodbye. I can't say I was heartbroken.

"I say, that was nice of you," Bovine said. "You could have ruined her reputation."

"Her reputation?" Aahz snarled. "What do you think it would do to *our* reputations if it got out that we went though all this without anything to show for our efforts?"

"That's not necessarily the case, Aahz," I said.

"Oh really? We're in a dimension with no money and we just turned all the gold to lead." Aahz said. "I'm not seeing much profit in that."

"Well, there's whatever Tananda shakes out of Glenda in return for our silence."

"That's payment for what she did. Not for our efforts."

I turned to Count Bovine.

"Check me on this." I said. "The deal was that I return for our help, we could have as much treasure as we could carry. Treasure, not specifically gold. Gold was just the obvious choice. Right?"

"That is correct," Bovine said.

"So how about one of the cow skulls from the energy room?"

"A cow skull?" Aahz frowned.

"Like, maybe, the one hanging on the wall with all the jewels on it?"

"That old dust-catcher? Is it still around?" Bovine seemed genuinely surprised. "Certainly. That seems fair. If you'll wait here a moment I'll fetch it for you."

He headed off in the direction of the skull room.

"You know, kid," Aahz said draping an arm across my shoulders, "there are times you show real promise."

"It's not much, but it's something." I said. "It seemed better that the other idea I had."

"What was that?"

"Turning the lead back into gold. The thing is, I don't know if anybody's ever tried that before."

Aahz was silent for a few moments.

"Apprentice," he said finally, his voice heavy, "it occurs to me you still have a lot to learn about magik."

Author's Biography

Robert (Lynn) Asprin was born in 1946. While he has written some stand alone novels such as *Cold Cash War*, *Tambu*, *The Bug Wars* and also the Duncan and Mallory Illustrated stories, Bob is best known for his series: The *Myth Adventures of Aahz and Skeeve*; the *Phule* novels; and, more recently, the *Time Scout* novels written with Linda Evans. He also edited the groundbreaking *Thieves World* anthologies with Lynn Abbey. His most recent collaboration is *License Invoked* written with Jody Lynn Nye. It is set in the French Quarter, New Orleans where he currently lives.

Myth Adventures One
1-892065-36-3
$16.00

They're Back!

Yes, Skeeve and Aahz are back!
They are also bringing the whole
Myth Adventures group with them!

Meisha Merlin is happy to announce the return of Robert Asprin and his magnificent *Myth Adventures* series. This new omnibus includes his first two books, *Another Fine Myth* and *Myth Conceptions*.

In *Another Fine Myth,* Skeeve, an apprentice wizard, meets the demon Aahz and though it's not love, or even like, at first sight they form a connection—saving their lives—between them. If having to share your life with a demon is not enough, Skeeve also adds a dragon and war unicorn as his accomplices.

In *Myth Conceptions,* Skeeve and Aahz have decided that taking on an entire army by themselves is something that they can do. The only catch is that they did not read the fine print. If they loose they know that the army will kill them. What they missed is that if they win, they will be executed! Even for two beings as talented as they are, getting out of this one with their lives could be a bit of a trial.

Myth Adventures Two
(*Myth Directions* & *Hit or Myth*)
February 2002

Myth Adventures Three
(*Myth-ing Persons* & *Little Myth Marker*)
June 2002

Something M.Y.T.H. Inc.
September 2002

From Jody Lynn Nye
(Robert Asprin's co-author on *License Invoked.*)

College. We all know what college is all about right? Either we have
been there ourselves, or know people who have and heard their
stories. Well, we were wrong!

In *Applied Mythology* Jody Lynn Nye shows us just what we missed
because of all that serious studying we did.

There are elves in the University Library! Also Leprechauns, sprites,
and a few other things. Keith Doyle is a business major who still
believes in myths and legends. When ever he has to write a paper for
a class he writes it on aliens and elves. Imagine his surprise and de-
light when he discovers the little people living in the sub-basement
of the old library. Also imagine his anger in realizing that they will be
forced to leave when the library is torn down for the modernization
of the campus. Finally imagine his horror when he realizes just who
has been leading this campaign for the modernization of the campus—him!

Fourth in the fun-loving contemporary fantasy series about Keith Doyle and the Little Folk he discovered living in the basement of his university library. *Advanced Mythology* finds Keith beginning graduate school while working for a Chicago advertising firm. He's writing ads for a top-secret product that will revolutionize personal electronics.

The Little Folk are being haunted by a malevolent presence that seems to be trying to drive them out of their house. At the same time, a stranger approaches Keith with a copy of a poster he designed that only the client and the firm are supposed to have seen—one that has hidden in it an invitation in the Little Folk's private language for Keith's long-dreamed-of party for all races of mystical beings.

Keith finds himself pitted against an industrial spy whose purpose is more sinister than he ever dreamed, while trying to protect his friends from mysterious outside forces.

It promises to be one heck of a party.

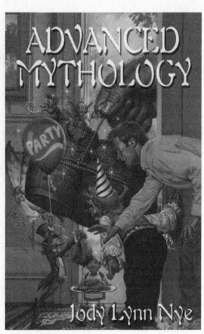

Advanced Mythology
Jody Lynn Nye

1-892065-46-0
Hard Cover $30

1-892065-47--9
Soft Cover $16

Cover by
Don Maitz

Come check out our web site for details on these Meisha Merlin authors!

Kevin J. Anderson

Robert Asprin

Robin Wayne Bailey

Edo van Belkom

Janet Berliner

Storm Constantine

Diane Duane

Sylvia Engdahl

Jim Grimsley

George Guthridge

Keith Hartman

Beth Hilgartner

P. C. Hodgell

Tanya Huff

Janet Kagan

Caitlin R. Kiernan

Lee Killough

George R. R. Martin

Lee Martindale

Jack McDevitt

Sharon Lee & Steve Miller

James A. Moore

Adam Niswander

Andre Norton

Jody Lynn Nye

Selina Rosen

Kristine Kathryn Rusch

Pamela Sargent

Michael Scott

William Mark Simmons

S. P. Somtow

Allen Steele

Mark Tiedeman

Freda Warrington

http://www.MeishaMerlin.com